S DUMAS, Alexandre
Fernande; the story of a
courtesan

DATE DUE

3/344

Fernande

Fernande

The Story of a Courtesan

by

Alexandre Dumas

Translated by
A. CRAIG BELL

ST. MARTIN'S PRESS
NEW YORK

© *English translation A. Craig Bell 1988*
First published in Great Britain 1988

ISBN 0 7090 3346 X

Robert Hale Limited
Clerkenwell House
Clerkenwell Green
London EC1R 0HT

Library of Congress Cataloging-in-Publication Data

Dumas, Alexandre, 1802-1870.
    Fernande.

    I. Title.
PQ2227.F213   1988   843'.7   88-30624
ISBN 0-312-02575-0

First published in Great Britain by Robert Hale Limited.

First U.S. Edition

10 9 8 7 6 5 4 3 2 1

Foreword

To the reader who knows only the Dumas of the historical romances this naturalistic novel of contemporary Parisian society with a courtesan as its 'heroine' will come as a surprise, and he will almost certainly wonder as to the reasons for his writing it. A brief explanation, then.

In 1842 Dumas wrote his second*, and one of his best, historical romances, namely *Le Chevalier d'Harmental* (better known in England as *The Conspirators*) after which, surprisingly, between that year and 1844 (year of the ever-famous *Les Trois Mousquetaires*) he wrote no less than seven novels of which three are historical romances, and negligible,† and four novels of contemporary life which are by no means negligible.‡ Of these latter, *Fernande* is by far the greatest. Written in 1843 it was occasioned by the publishers of a work to be given the title of *La Grande Ville* and planned as a study of Paris and its society, who approached Dumas with a request for a contribution dealing with the shadier aspects of them. The result was the atonishing article *Filles, Lorettes et Courtisanes*, undertaken as he tells us in the preface, 'reluctantly, and only because no one else dared.'

In the course of his researches into this class of women he discovered that a surprisingly large number had been led to take up their sordid way of life after having been seduced

* His first was *Acté*, set in the time of Nero.
† Viz. *Sylvandire, Ascanio* and *Cécile*.
‡ Viz. *Georges, Amaury, Gabriel Lambert* and *Fernande*.

while young and inexperienced by older men, and in many cases had come from respectable and even aristocratic families. This fact led him to consider making just such a woman the centrepiece of a novel, and from this idea he created Fernande – a woman who had come from an aristocratic family, had received a good education and showed talent in art and music. But seduced and betrayed by a comrade-in-arms of her dead father who had asked him to take his place and be her 'guardian', and left alone and unbefriended to live as best she could, in a kind of desperate revenge on herself and society for her degradation she makes herself a high-class courtesan. And this life of hectic factitious gaiety is led by her until she meets the young, rich, handsome Baron Maurice de Barthèle. Forestalling by a decade the similar situation and affair of Armand Duval and Marguerite Gautier in his son's *La Dame aux Camélias* (in the preface to his novel Dumas *fils* acknowledges his debt to his father's creation), Fernande falls deeply in love with him as he with her although he is married, becomes his mistress and for his sake puts her former way of life behind her. With what result the novel narrates. In Dumas's own words:

> Our story is not so much a narrative of events as a drama of analysis. It is a moral autopsy we are undertaking. And just as in the soundest body there is some organic lesion through which sooner or later death strikes, so the noblest hearts hide secret weaknesses which serve to remind us that man is a compound of noble sentiments and petty actions.

While the courtesan Fernande is the keystone of the narrative, the other characters are drawn with consummate skill – in particular Madame de Barthèle with her goodness of heart and unorganised mind; while the waspish Madame de Neuilly is delineated with the observation and acidity of Jane Austen or Trollope.

In fact, the novel is a revelation of a new facet of Dumas's genius; and that it is authentic Dumas and not by any other hand is manifest to anyone who has read his sixty-odd novels to any extent. Every page is stamped with his style. Furthermore there is a sure and certain imprint to be found in the discussion (typically French, this) over Madame de Barthèle's luncheon table on the state of contemporary art, music and literature in the course of which, replying to Madame de Neuilly's horror at her (Fernande's) confessed admiration of Shakespeare: 'That barbarian,' Fernande replies, 'That barbarian is the being who has created the most after God,' and goes on to tell her that all women should have a cult of gratitude to him for his creation of the most admirable types of their sex in Desdemona, Miranda and Ophelia.

Dumas was proud of his Shakespearian dictum, which became famous, and which he was to repeat in his *Mes Mémoires* (1852-55). To savour to the full the allusion and atmosphere the reader should know that until the visit to Paris in 1827 of the English Shakespearean company under Kemble, in the minds of the French theatre-minded public and critics the Bard was indeed regarded as the 'barbarian' of Voltaire. But to the young militant Romantics Shakespeare completed a literary revolution begun by Scott and Byron. Two more than the rest were moved and inspired by the English players' performances: one was Alexandre Dumas, the other Hector Berlioz. The latter was so far carried away and so desperately in love with the Irish actress Henrietta Smithson, that he was said to have declared, 'I will marry Juliet and write my greatest symphony on the play!'* Dumas wrote differently but equally ecstatically: 'Imagine a man blind from birth suddenly receiving the gift of sight and discovering a whole world of which he had no idea existed ... I realised that Shakespeare's works contained as much variety as the works of all the other playwrights combined, and recognised that next to the Creator himself, he had created more than any other being ....'

* Five years later, in fact, Harriet was married to Berlioz.

Later he was quoted as saying, 'I owe every Englishman a debt of gratitude for Scott, Byron and Shakespeare.' English readers should surely be grateful to the French writer for those words.

A.C.B.

One

One

It was May 1835 and one of those heart-easing first spring days when Paris begins to be depopulated by all who, unless chained to the capital by necessity, leave it to enjoy the fresh verdure of the countryside which, with us, comes so late and lasts so short a time.

A woman in her mid-forties, but whose face still retained something of her once remarkable beauty, whose dress displayed her perfect taste, whose gestures and whole bearing denoted her breeding, was standing on the verandah of a charming country house situated at the end of the village of Fontenay-aux-Roses, preparing to greet a carriage drawn by two superb chestnut horses which drew up at the foot of the verandah steps.

'Ah! So here you are at last, my dear Count!' She greeted a man of some sixty years who sprang off the footboard and up the steps with an affected lightness of foot. 'I have been waiting for you with the utmost impatience. I swear to you that this must be the tenth time I have been here on the look-out for you.'

'My dear Baroness,' replied the count, kissing her hand with an air of studied gallantry, 'I ordered my carriage the moment Germain delivered your note, that is to say at eight o'clock while I was still in bed. It is still only nine, so you can see I have not wasted any time. Now then, tell me, what is it all about? I am at your orders.'

'Good! In that case send your carriage back. I am keeping you.'

'What! For a whole day?'

'And the evening into the bargain. Surely you remember that in my note I told you we needed your presence here urgently.'

However strong his self-control, Monsieur de Montgiroux – such was the count's name – could not repress an involuntary grimace. For he recollected just then that he had an engagement for the opera to which he was looking forward with no little eagerness.

'Oh, *mon Dieu*! that's quite impossible, my dear,' he hastened to excuse himself. 'Today is the seventh and I am on the committee of a commission which is meeting to discuss a possible change in a law –'

'Then it must be discussed without your presence, my dear Count,' the baroness interpolated. 'Surely the illness of our invalid is more important than that.'

'But my dear Eugénie,' cried Monsieur de Montgiroux with an impatience still more marked than before, 'I am not a doctor.'

'Monsieur le comte, it is a question of my son, your niece's husband; of our Maurice, in a word.'

'Is he no better then?' Monsieur de Montgiroux asked in a softer tone.

'Yesterday the doctor told us he was worse, much worse.'

'Ah! *Mon Dieu*! I never thought his situation could become so serious.'

'For the simple reason that it is a week since we saw anything of you, ingrate that you are!'

'But what is the matter with the boy?' the count asked.

'To begin with it was just a state of acute melancholy; then it became profound languor, leading to an indifference towards everyone and everything. Finally, in spite of all our care, he became feverish, and now he is delirious.'

'That's extraordinary in a man,' the count remarked, more anxiously. 'And what is the cause of this melancholy and fever?'

'We don't know, but we have hopes of a cure. The doctor, who is not only a doctor but a friend of Maurice's, is confident he can cure him. Can't you understand what that means to a mother?'

'So there's no immediate danger, then?'

'It merely means that there is more hope today than yesterday.' The baroness took him up, seeing through the purpose of his questioning. 'But it is precisely this improvement which makes it essential for you to stay.'

'But my dear, that is really quite impossible,' the count insisted with another grimace.

'Really, I cannot believe you can, for a moment, weigh the importance of our son's health against a meeting such as you talk about.'

'I concede, my dear, I concede,' the count said, capitulating in principle, but adding, 'I will give up the whole of today to you and tomorrow morning. I only ask that you free me for three hours this evening.'

'Since you ask for it I suppose I must. But you know, Count, if I were younger and disposed to jealousy …'

'Well?'

'Well, you would make me pass a very unhappy day with your eternal preoccupation.'

'I, preoccupied?'

'To such a degree that you don't show the least uneasiness about the state of mind of Clotilde and me in all this trouble.'

'Pardon, my dear, but as a peer of the realm and a citizen of some note, I feel obliged to contribute my share to these meetings.'

'Really, my dear Count, how you do go on!' Madame de Barthèle took him up with withering irony. 'Citizen indeed! If you go on speaking in this way, given a couple more revolutions like the last one, I foresee you dying a rabid Jacobin!'

This conversation, as we have stated, took place on the verandah of Madame de Barthèle's château. Having won him over to stay, at any rate for the rest of the day, she signed to him to follow her, and after wending her way along various passages well known to them both, she led him to the room where the invalid was lying. But just as they were about to go in, a young woman emerged suddenly but silently from an adjoining ante-room and barred their entrance.

'Ssh! Silence!' she warned with a look of fear and yet of importance. 'He's sleeping, and the doctor says he mustn't be disturbed.'

'Asleep!' cried Madame de Barthèle with an accent of maternal joy.

'We hope so, at least. His eyes are closed and he seems less agitated.'

'Poor Maurice!' said his mother, stifling a deep sigh. 'We must obey doctor's orders,' she went on. 'Let us go into the drawing-room,' she added, taking the count's arm. 'We can talk freely there, and I have so much to tell you.'

'Well, Uncle,' said Clotilde in a tone of tender reproach, 'haven't you any greeting for me?'

'But aren't you coming with us?' the count asked as he kissed her forehead.

'No, I shall stay in this little room where I can be near him and hear if he needs me.'

'She's never been away from him,' Madame de Barthèle observed. 'She's wonderful!'

'But can't you let us see the doctor, at least?' her uncle suggested. 'I would like a few words with him.'

'Of course, Uncle. I'll send him along to you.' On which he went with Madame de Barthèle to the drawing-room.

* * *

Before proceeding further with our story, we must inform the reader regarding the two persons we have put before them and whom we shall shortly rejoin in the drawing-room.

Monsieur le comte de Montgiroux, sixty years of age and a peer of France, had long been the lover of Madame de Barthèle. They had never married for the reason that she, at the age of twenty, had been pressed by her family into what they considered an advantageous *mariage de convenance* to a Monsieur de Barthèle. Deeply in love with the count, she had frankly confessed as much to her husband before the wedding and demanded complete freedom. By a happy chance, Monsieur de Barthèle was a man of the old eighteenth-century school, with a similar affair on his hands. He appreciated his wife's frankness, and an agreement was reached between them which gave each absolute freedom. So that to the world in general and their relations in particular, their marriage was regarded as a great success. After a year of marriage Madame de Barthèle gave birth to a baby boy. The child was brought up as though he had been his own by Monsieur de Barthèle and was given his name. Fifteen years later that worthy gentleman died, and his wife then entered the paradise of widowhood without ever having had, as was said at that period, to endure the purgatory of wedlock.

It was then that one of her relations, a certain Madame de Neuilly, an embittered spinster and a woman of enforced and self-proclaimed virtue who had always envied her cousin's marriage and wealth, had urged her to enter into a second marriage, in the name of morality, with the count. But on Madame de Barthèle mentioning this to her lover, he had only replied in the famous words of Nicholas Chamfort: 'I have thought of it myself, my dear, but if we were to get married, where the devil should I spend my evenings?' And this naive response was perfectly in character with a man who for the past twenty-five years had spent his evenings anywhere but at home, and was perfectly understood and accepted by his mistress.

They had not, therefore, married, and their son, Maurice, grew up in ignorance of all this and alongside Clotilde, his cousin, daughter of the late Vicomte de Montgiroux, younger brother of the count.

Such was the situation in the spring of 1835 when our narrative opens. Clotilde was seventeen and Maurice twenty-four. Growing up together, as it were, it was considered the obvious and right thing by respective guardians and relations to persuade the young couple into marriage. As they were fond of each other this was found to be no difficult matter, although, be it said, whereas Clotilde was very much in love with Maurice, his feelings for his cousin were more those of a brother for a sister.

Maurice had developed into a handsome young man excelling in all sports and yet, at the same time, was a connoisseur of the arts. He was also a popular man of the world with his male associates and in the various Parisian clubs of which he was a noted member. It resulted from this that Clotilde found herself frequently left alone, but without any serious grounds for dissension, since Maurice's name had never been mixed with any sort of scandal or with any other woman.

Then suddenly all that was changed. Overnight Maurice became a different and strange person. From being gay and lively, he became first moody, sad-faced and uncommunicative, then melancholy; and finally fell into a state of complete apathy and depression ending in his taking to his bed and refusing all attempts by his wife and mother to rouse him. Deeply concerned they called in their doctor, Gaston, a youngish practitioner who was not only a doctor but a family friend. He saw at once that the source of the mysterious illness was one of those which the sufferer has neither wish nor will to cure: a mental illness, in fact, the cause of which the patient would not reveal.

It was precisely at this stage that Madame de Barthèle had summoned her former lover to her side to ask for advice and to ease her mind over the condition of their son. So it was that, on finding herself tête-à-tête with Monsieur de Montgiroux in the drawing-room, at his request to be told the facts about Maurice, the distraught woman was only too anxious to impart what little she knew. But the truth was that Madame de Barthèle, while having been endowed by nature with a kind heart, had been equally endowed with the least methodical mind imaginable, so that her conversation proceeded by illogical leaps and bounds, only arriving at their conclusions by innumerable deviations.

Thus, her first expressions to the count were all about the devotion of Clotilde towards her husband and the words of the doctor. But eventually brought back to the point by the somewhat restive and impatient count, she continued: 'For Clotilde and for me, as you can well appreciate, my dear Count, Maurice's life is everything.'

'Of course, of course,' he hastened to agree.

'But we are defeated by this mysterious illness and in the depths of despair. We keep asking ourselves and wondering what it can be that brings about such a state in a young man who has health, wealth, good looks, character – everything a young man can desire in fact. Yet whatever it is, it is bringing him to death's door.'

'Really! I had no idea that things were as bad as that,' the count observed.

'The doctor – he's Maurice's friend, Gaston, you know – took me aside and asked me if I knew anything about Maurice which could bring about any profound grief, for he is convinced there is such a cause. He has known Maurice for ten years, and he insists there is no physical reason which could cause his illness, apparently a mena-meno-meni ...'

'Meningitis?'

'Yes, that's it. Acute meningitis, that's what Gaston said it was.'

'This could be serious,' the count remarked. 'Perhaps if I could talk with him –'

'And do you suppose you would get anything from him when I, his mother, and Clotilde, have failed? Besides, it would be useless. Thanks to a stupid valet, we have begun to see daylight in the mystery.'

'A valet?' the count echoed brusquely.

'Yes, a valet. Isn't it strange how these things come about! One is tempted to believe there is a Providence over and above our acts, Count.'

'Well, and this valet?' the count repeated impatiently, not being interested in the good lady's philosophical reflections.

'He made his way into Maurice's room before anyone could prevent him, and announced, again before he could be stopped, that two friends of my son, Léon de Vaux and Fabien de Rieulle had come to see him. You know them, I believe.'

'Yes, and unfortunately through not very savoury reports,' the count replied. 'Two young society men who keep dubious company, I gather. If I were you, my dear, I would forbid Maurice to entertain these gentlemen.'

'Come, come, my dear Count!' remonstrated the baroness. 'How can I be expected to tell a man of twenty-seven, even if he is my son, who his friends must or must not be? In any case, Léon and Fabien aren't friends of yesterday. He has known them these past six or seven years.'

'Nevertheless, I *still* say they are bad company.'

'Bad company, bad company!' rejoined the baroness, drawn yet again into side issues a hundred miles outside the subject, as was her wont. 'How do you know that?' she demanded. 'Not because you associate with them, I hope.'

The count compressed his lips in an involuntary movement, like a minister who has unintentionally committed himself to a dangerous truth in the flow of his speech; but immediately controlling himself the peer rejoined, smiling, 'I, madame, at my sixty years of age!'

'They say men are as old as they feel, monsieur.'

'My dear,' he said, anxious to avoid quibbling and to sidetrack her jealous tongue, 'you are forgetting it is our Maurice's health we are concerned with and nothing else.'

'All the same, if I were given to jealousy,' she went on, woman-like, unable to bring herself to overlooking personal issues, 'I would hazard a guess that your opinion of these young men is not so disinterested as you would like to make out. But we will let that pass. It is all a question of Maurice at the moment. And despite your opinion of Messieurs de Vaux and de Rieulle, as soon as he heard the valet mention their names, he seemed to come to life, and told him to admit them. And yet to all the questions and anxious watching of his wife and mother he has been blind and deaf. It is incredible!'

'Their names, it seems then, have produced something of a revolution in his state,' the peer remarked gravely.

'Precisely! And that, whatever you may say about them, makes me more sympathetic towards them.'

'Continue, my dear. This is becoming interesting.'

'You may well say that, my dear Count. Maurice then ordered the valet to tell them to come in right away. I looked at the doctor, and he whispered to me, "This is a good move. Leave him alone with his friends. Quite possibly, knowing more about his social life than we do, something of his secret may come out in their conversation. We can question them when they leave."

'I took Clotilde's hand and the three of us left the room and entered the little cabinet adjoining the bedroom just as the two young men entered it.

' "Now then, Doctor," I said to Gaston, "would it be in order, do you think, if we were to stay hidden here and listen to this talk?"

' "In view of the gravity of the circumstances," he said, "I think we might permit ourselves that little indiscretion." '

'And Clotilde stayed with you?' the count said, raising his eyebrows.

'Yes. I wanted her to go away, but she refused. "He is my husband," she said "if he is your son. I am staying with you to listen, and whatever we overhear, whatever the secret, don't worry. I shan't make a scene." So she held my hand and the three of us stayed there and listened.'

'Go on, go on!' exclaimed the count, a hint of sarcasm in his voice. 'Really, what I am hearing has all the improbability and yet all the interest of a novel.'

'Well, what we overheard', Madame de Barthèle resumed 'was something quite dreadful. Léon de Vaux began it by jeering at the poor boy in such a mocking way that it was all I could do not to break in and send him packing. Then Fabien took him up with: "There's no help for it. He's got it beyond hope!" and laughed.

'Then Maurice made everything horribly clear to us by his reply. "That's true," he confessed, "but I can't do anything about it. She's the only woman I have ever really loved, and when she broke it off with me something seemed to die in me."

' "But my dear fellow," Fabien took him up, "I've loved her too. Everyone's loved her! But when you succeeded me in her favours I didn't lie down and die from it. On the contrary, we agreed to be just friends, and so we are." You can imagine poor Clotilde's feelings, listening to all that. I felt her hand becoming hot as she gripped mine and I could see she was as pale as death. I signed to her she should go, but she only shook her head, and went on listening.

' "Impossible!" Maurice almost shouted. "Impossible! After having possessed her I could never be just friends and see her become the mistress of someone else. I couldn't bear it. I would kill him, whoever it might be."

' "What!" Fabien exclaimed. "Fight a duel over that creature!" '

'But what woman are they talking about?' cried Monsieur de Montgiroux impatiently.

'That's what we don't know yet,' replied the baroness. 'Either from chance or precaution they never mentioned her name.'

'Maurice in love with another woman and not his wife, not my poor niece!' cried the count. 'And now Clotilde knows about it! Aren't you furious?'

'What would be the good of that, Monsieur Rigorist? Passion is a disease which attacks we don't know how, and goes we don't know why.'

'Yes, maybe. But surely Maurice can't be ill like this because of a love affair.'

'All the same, he is. Ah! here is the doctor. If you don't believe me, ask him.'

'Well, Doctor,' the count greeted Gaston's appearance, 'do you really believe that my nephew's illness is caused by a passing love affair?'

'No, Count,' replied Gaston, 'not a passing affair, but a real passion.'

'But a passion, a real passion for a woman of her kind?'

'There is reality and illusion,' rejoined the doctor.

'But do you think, then, this woman, whoever she is, is perhaps not all she is made out to be?'

'In the first place,' the doctor replied, 'I don't know her, nor do any of us. But as you probably know, Monsieur de

Rieulle has the reputation for speaking lightly of women's characters.'

'But that isn't what astonishes me,' observed Madame de Barthèle.

'What does astonish you, then?' demanded the count.

'What really amazes me is that any woman loved by Maurice, who is young, handsome, well-off and has all the graces, should deceive him for any other man, I don't care who he may be. This is what makes me believe that this woman is not worthy of his love.'

'But, my dear,' remonstrated the count, 'you talk as if Maurice was single and unattached. Think of poor Clotilde.'

'Clotilde has been marvellous through it all. Hasn't she, Doctor? She threw herself into my arms with "We will save him, won't we, in spite of everything?" I tell you, it is only women who know what devoted love is.'

'Ill through love – Maurice!' murmured the count, unable to overcome his astonishment.

'Certainly, ill through love,' asserted Madame de Barthèle with a show of maternal belief that was part tragic, part comic. 'What is there astonishing in that? Don't we hear every day of some lover who has blown his brains out or thrown himself into the river because of a love affair?'

'But it seems incredible to me that a man can bring himself to such a state because of a woman,' the count remarked.

'No, Count, it is far from incredible, at least to us medical practitioners. Why shouldn't a violent emotion of despair produce, especially in the case of an organism as finely balanced and sensitive as that of Maurice, a lethargy, a disorder as desperate as that caused by a sword or a pistol shot? Go and examine him, and you will find his face drawn and pale, with sclerosis of the eye, his pulse fluctuating – all the symptoms, in fact, of acute meningitis, or in more common words, brain fever. And this brain fever has been brought on by a profound grief. So, what we have to do is to combat this grief in the same way it was caused. Short of doing this, he can die as surely as if he had blown his brains out.'

'And what is this remedy you aim to bring about?'

'Oh, *mon Dieu*! there's nothing new about it. In fact it is hundreds of years old. Do you know the tale of Stratonice and young Demetrius?'

'Yes.'

'Well, in the same way, we must bring the object of his passion before his eyes; and since, it seems, the lady in question is not notorious for her virtue, there's every chance she will be able to cure the illness of which she is the cause.'

'But how are you going to bring about this cure? Maurice, it seems, is too ill to leave his bed.'

'In which case,' observed Madame de Barthèle, 'she must come to him.'

'What!' exclaimed the count in a tone of horror. 'Bring this woman here! – a woman whose name we don't even know! A courtesan!'

'She can be and be called whatever she likes, provided she brings my son back to normal life.'

'But what will everyone think and say when they know you are harbouring a woman of her reputation under your roof?'

'They can think and say what they please. It is not "everyone" (as you say) who will cure my son, and this woman probably can. That is the whole answer.'

'You are determined on it, then?'

'Irrevocably.'

'And the doctor approves?'

'I not only approve, I advise it,' put in Gaston.

'In that case, I have no more to say, except to ask when this dramatic scene is to take place.'

'Why do you ask, Count?'

'So as to be in Paris on the occasion, that is all.'

'Well, I have to tell you it is to take place today, and the reason I asked you to come in the first place was so that you could be with us and support us when it occurs.'

'But, my dear!' cried the count in consternation, 'Think of my position as a peer. Subject as I am to the scrutiny of public opinion –'

'Ssh!' interrupted the baroness. 'Here's Clotilde.' In fact, at that moment the young woman entered the room.

Two

Two

Clotilde had come to tell her uncle that Maurice was awake and that he could now pay the invalid a visit. Looking at his niece, Monsieur de Montgiroux observed that she was pale, but to all appearances calm and resigned. But the count, being a peer of the realm and less given to emotion than the baroness, could not blind himself to what he considered an indescribably shocking contravention of the social code in permitting a courtesan and former mistress of a husband to be entertained by his wife and mother in their home. Not only so, but an unreasoning fear made him dread meeting this unknown woman, above all in the company of the baroness. He had attempted to get out of it; but Madame de Barthèle, falling back on their former intimacy and her authority, had almost forced him to stay. Moreover, she was beginning to have her suspicions as to the sentiments of her one-time lover and to question him with some warmth when Clotilde appeared on the scene.

In response to her announcement both rose and followed her, the count racking his brains all the while as to how he could decently get himself out of the embarrassing situation. The sight of a tilbury entering the courtyard drew from Madame de Barthèle an exclamation: 'Ah! here is Monsieur de Rieulle!' she cried. 'Now perhaps we shall have some news.'

The count saw his opportunity. 'Go back to your husband,' he said to his niece. 'I will join you in a minute or two. I want to go with Madame de Barthèle and find out what is happening.' Saying which he hastily followed the baroness, determined not to allow her to be alone with the newcomer.

The latter was a young man in his late twenties and, to a superficial observer, of extreme good looks and elegance.

'Well, Monsieur de Rieulle,' Madame de Barthèle greeted him, 'what have you to tell us? Speak! We are longing to know.'

But as the young man opened his mouth to reply he caught sight of the count. The baroness perceived his hesitation. 'Oh, you can speak freely before the count,' she assured him. 'He knows all about our little plot.'

Still looking at Monsieur de Montgiroux, Fabien's hesitation changed to a look of astonishment. 'Well, madame,' he said at last, 'I think we can say everything is turning out as we hoped. *The person in question* has accepted our invitation to come and see the house.'

'But when can we expect her?' the baroness enquired anxiously.

'The rendezvous is for this very morning, madame, and she should be arriving any time now.' As he spoke, Fabien observed the count closely; but he had had the time to assume the demeanour of a man versed in the rôle of politician, and remained impassive.

'She raised no objections, then?' Madame de Barthèle asked.

'No, madame. We simply told her it was an invitation to see a charming country house that was for sale. An excursion, in fact. Léon de Vaux is accompanying her, and I am sure he will have succeeded in telling her the real reason for the visit by the time they arrive.'

'But monsieur,' the count demanded in a voice which despite his attempt to make the question nonchalant, betrayed his anxiety, 'what is the name of this person, if you please?'

'What! Do you not know?' Fabien exclaimed in obvious surprise.

'Not at all. How should I?'

'She is called Madame Ducoudray,' Fabien replied coolly with a slight and ironical bow.

'Madame Ducoudray,' repeated the count with obvious relief. 'No, I have never heard of her.' And he breathed freely once more. Observing this Fabien smiled imperceptibly.

'Dear lady,' said the count to Madame de Barthèle, 'now that we are certain of the arrival of our lady magician, I leave you to talk with Monsieur de Rieulle while I go and have a word with the invalid.'

'But you will stay with us, I hope.'

'Of course, since that is your wish. Only you will, I hope, free me for an hour or two this evening as I asked earlier, you may remember.'

'Certainly, Count.'

'Thank you. You will not mind, then, if I send a little note to tell them I shall be coming.'

'By all means do so.'

The count then seated himself at a little bureau on which were pens, notepaper, envelopes and ink for household use, and taking a sheet of perfumed vellum and a pen he wrote hastily, 'This evening, 8'clock, at the Opera, *ma toute belle*' Then, after a quick glance in the direction of his hostess, he put the *billet-doux* in an envelope, sealed and addressed it, and after giving orders about the delivery of it, took his way to Maurice's room.

Left alone with her son's friend, the baroness felt more at ease and began to sound him with her customary loquacity. 'So,' she began, 'we shall really see this beautiful Madame Ducoudray? She is beautiful, I understand.'

'More than that. She is bewitching.'

'Really! And is Madame Ducoudray really her name?'

'That is what we have decided to call her under the circumstances. Under such a name she can be accepted in your house by all and sundry.'

'But her real name – what is that?'

'If you mean her family name, I don't believe she has told it to anyone.'

'I see! No doubt she will turn out to be the daughter of some *grand seigneur*!' said the baroness with a laugh.

'That could well be,' Fabien admitted. 'In fact I have thought as much myself more than once.'

'In that case I am not asking for the name inscribed in the armorial of France, but the one she is generally known by.'

'It is Fernande.'

'And this name is ... well known, you say?'

'Very well known, madame – as that of the woman most *à la mode* in Paris.'

'She must indeed be all you say to inspire such dreadful passions. Now I begin to understand why my son should fall so terribly in love with her. What I do not understand, though, is how and why she resisted him.'

'It is not that she resisted him, madame; it is simply that one day he found her door barred to him.'

'But I find that still more astonishing. What do you suppose was the reason for her caprice? It can't be from mercenary motives, surely, for Maurice is well-off and generous.'

'I don't believe such to be the case, madame. I am sure Fernande is above such sordid considerations.'

'Do you know, Monsieur de Rieulle, what you tell me of her gives me the greatest curiosity to meet her.'

'You will have that pleasure very shortly, madame.'

'And that reminds me to consult you as to the best manner in which to receive her. My idea – and all you have told me about her confirms my belief – is that we should try to forget her dubious social position and treat her as we would a veritable and respectable Madame Ducoudray.'

'I am happy to be able to agree with you, madame.'

'From your description of her I feel sure that a studied politeness on my part will conduce to a reciprocal attitude on hers. In which case no one could find anything improper in her visit. Though heaven forbid my cousin, Madame de Neuilly, should take it into her head to drop in on us! You know her, I believe, Monsieur de Rieulle.'

Fabien nodded with a meaningful smile.

'Yes, I understand you,' the baroness said, smiling in her turn. 'She is the most prying, mischief-making woman on God's earth, and the last person we would want here at this time.'

'Granted, madame. But everything, it seems to me, should pass off smoothly. What astonishes me most in all this, though, if I may say so without being indiscreet, is the willingness of Madame Maurice de Barthèle to consent in taking the cause of her husband's condition – in fact her rival – into her house.'

'But in the circumstances, monsieur, what else could she do? Make herself a widow out of revenge? You see, she adores Maurice, and we women, you know, can adore men with all their faults, and even because of them. They were brought up together, and her love for Maurice is something real and durable, and not one of those debasing passions such as he obviously has for this woman.'

Fabien could not repress a smile on learning from Maurice's mother the truth of his relationship with his wife – a truth which he had long suspected, namely, that their marriage, on his side at least, had been primarily one of family self-interest; and this confirmation served to strengthen his secret intentions, for Fabien had intentions.

A sudden noise made Madame de Barthèle turn round to see Clotilde enter. 'Oh, *mon Dieu*!' exclaimed the baroness, 'What is it? He isn't worse, I trust.'

'No, madame. But uncle has asked me to leave him alone with Maurice and the doctor, so I came down to join you.'

She responded to Fabien's polite bow with an equally polite curtsey.

'Very well, then.' the baroness said. 'You can relax, my dear' she pursued. 'This lady – you know whom I mean – this Madame Ducoudray, has agreed to come, and should be here any minute.'

Clotilde lowered her eyes and gave an involuntary sigh.

'You see', Madame de Barthèle said in an aside to Fabien,

'how grief has affected her health too, poor dear child!'

The young man cast a questioning glance at Clotilde, and this examination, though brief, was sufficient to convince him that Madame de Barthèle was mistaken. True, she was pale, but her pallor might equally be the result of fatigue from watching over her husband as from grief; and even because of it he thought he had never seen his friend's wife looking so attractive. So, while she stood there with her eyes lowered, and while the baroness went on declaring how deeply she was suffering, Fabien found a certain charm in studying the naive young woman (she was barely twenty) for whom three years of marriage had scarcely broken her pristine innocence; and he couldn't help reflecting on the bizarre caprices of the human heart which could transform the cool husband into the madly impassioned lover of Fernande.

But Madame de Barthèle left the young couple little time for sighs and reflection, and with her eternal garrulity went on: 'Well then, here you are, dear Clotilde. You were there when your uncle entered the poor boy's room, I take it. Did he seem to know your uncle?'

'I hardly know, for he never so much as turned to look at him. And when uncle spoke to him he didn't even answer.'

'You see, then, Monsieur Fabien,' the baroness addressed the young man, 'in what a sad state our poor Maurice is. And surely nothing we can do to restore him to health is too much.'

Fabien gave a nod of assent.

'So what did your uncle do then?' the baroness continued.

'He spoke to the doctor, then he asked me to leave them together.'

'And didn't Maurice notice your departure?'

'No!' Clotilde had to confess with a blush and a second sigh.

'Madame,' Fabien said to the baroness in a voice low enough to preserve an air of mystery but clear enough to be heard by Clotilde, 'don't you think it might be advisable to let Maurice know what is happening; I mean, to warn him, without mentioning names, he is about to receive a visit from a beautiful young woman? It is my opinion that the sudden appearance of this woman who is the cause of his condition might be too much of a shock, and perhaps bring on a dangerous crisis.'

'Yes, indeed, Monsieur Fabien,' Madame de Barthèle replied. 'You are right. Dear Clotilde,' she pursued, raising her voice, 'Monsieur de Rieulle has just suggested –'

'I heard what Monsieur de Rieulle said,' Clotilde put in.

'Well, what is your opinion?'

'You have more experience in these things than I have, madame, and quite honestly I hesitate to give an opinion on the matter.'

'For my part,' Madame de Barthèle opined, 'I am in complete agreement with Monsieur Fabien. This is what I propose – that I join Monsieur de Montgiroux and the doctor, and instead of speaking softly and taking precautions against disturbing Maurice as we have done so far, we discuss this proposed visit from the unknown lady openly, so that he can hear. And to encourage him to have suspicions as to her identity I will go on about her beauty and youth, and perhaps even hint at her – well, you know – a rumoured wantonness.'

Whereupon, anxious to carry out her plan, Madame de Barthèle moved towards the door. Clotilde made to follow her. But the baroness stopped her with, 'No, no! Wait here, my dear. Upon reflection I hardly think it wise for you to be there. Knowing you are there Maurice will hardly dare to ask questions about this woman, which is what we want him to do. I feel at bottom, you know, that in his heart he is very much ashamed of his conduct towards you.'

'Oh, madame!' murmured Clotilde, blushing with embarrassment before Fabien.

'See how lovely she is!' the baroness exclaimed with her usual careless freedom. 'Really! I can't understand Maurice. It is ridiculous of him! Do you know, my dear, when he gets back to health I will go so far as to advise you to give him something to think about in return!'

'How do you mean, madame?' her daughter-in-law demanded, her clear blue eyes expressing her youthful innocence.

'How? If you really do not know, my dear, I will tell you myself at the appropriate time!'

Although the young girl tried not to show it, the conversation was becoming displeasing to her. Fabien, with the perception of a consummate psychologist, understood her feelings perfectly.

'By the way, Monsieur Fabien,' the baroness continued without seeing how her daughter-in-law was suffering, 'is this woman dark or fair?'

'Dark, madame.'

'Really! How can he fall for a brunette when he has under his eyes such an adorable blonde? Tall or short?'

'Of medium height, but perfectly proportioned.'

'And her taste in dress?'

'Exquisitely simple, and simply exquisite.'

'So! I see you are an admirer! Well, I leave you two together. Let me know, Clotilde, the moment you see Madame Ducoudray's carriage. Incidentally, Monsieur de Rieulle, how will she arrive?'

'Probably in her barouche. The weather is too fine for her to come in her brougham, I should say.'

'Indeed! So she has all these different conveyances, this princess?'

'Yes, madame. And as a matter of fact they are cited for their elegance.'

'*Mon Dieu! Mon Dieu!*' exclaimed the baroness raising her hands as she left the room. 'The times we live in!'

Fabien and Clotilde were left alone together.

*　　*　　*

As we have already intimated, this tête-à-tête was what Fabien had hoped and manoeuvred for. A brief description of the young man is necessary for the full understanding of his objective. A good-looking man of nearly thirty, his looks belied his years, and at a cursory glance one would account him a proper model of a certain type of Parisian society, so that only a closer examination and knowledge revealed that subtle distinction between an acquired and a natural breeding as shown in comparison between him and his friend Maurice de Barthèle. Fabien had benefited from all that education and society can give a man as distinct from what birth and nature bequeath. Fabien had made the mistake of seeking the friendship of Maurice, a fact which proved unfortunate for him since in every way the latter showed himself to be his superior: in manner, dress, sport, conversation, everything which brought them together. Maurice's horses in their races proved better than his; his equipages were considered more elegant; in friendly sword-play Maurice was nearly always the victor. Although he took his inferiority with apparent nonchalance, Fabien hid underneath it a secret determination to get his own back some day in some way or another. In this bizarre situation he fancied he saw his chance.

The extreme embarrassment manifested by Clotilde on finding herself alone with him seemed to Fabien to be a favourable augury. As a man experienced in the art of seduction he foresaw at once the advantage to be accrued from Madame de Barthèle's plan to bring Maurice's former mistress to his house. As the first step to ingratiate himself with his friend's wife he had taken care to ensure that it should be Léon who actually brought Clotilde's rival into the domestic domain, in itself a humiliation for the young wife, leaving him, Fabien, guiltless and, into the bargain, free to get to know her and to begin working on her emotions.

So now, seeing her embarrassment, Fabien was too adroit not to leave it to her to break an emotional silence which he felt to be more expressive than any words might be.

'Monsieur,' she began at last, 'while waiting for Madame de Barthèle to return, perhaps you would care to have a look at some of our flowers which I believe are quite rare, and which our gardener tends with great pride.'

'I am at your orders, madame,' Fabien responded with a respectful bow. On his reply, and as if to escape from her emotions, Clotilde turned and led the way out of the *salon*, through the billiards room and so to the conservatory.

'Here are some lovely plants,' she said, looking at a collection of them with an attention too studied to be natural. 'Our gardener is very proud of them. But it seems to me that since my husband's illness they appear to be out of sorts. To tell the truth, I have not been in here for over a week.'

Still Fabien took care not to speak, telling himself that silence on his part would in all probability force the young woman to come round to the subject he desired. She no doubt understood his intention, for she raised her eyes from the plants to look at him; but meeting his, and the unmistakable ardour in them, she hastily lowered hers and turned her attention to the plant again. Then, realising that the all-important subject had to be raised sooner or later, and plucking up her courage, she led the way to a sort of divan, and after seating herself and signing to Fabien to join her, she began tentatively with: 'Monsieur de Rieulle, you have shown a good deal of enthusiasm in telling us about this Madame Ducoudray ...'

'Enthusiasm, madame?' Fabien interpolated. 'Certainly not. Permit me to disagree with you there.'

'And yet I heard you speak of her to Madame de Barthèle not only as a very distinguished person but as being exceptionally beautiful. And in fact this has helped me to try to understand Maurice's passion for her.'

Fabien saw that the conversation was taking the turn he desired and which seemed most favourable for his projects.

'Believe me, madame,' he replied. 'I understand and sympathise with your trouble. Now if only Maurice had listened to me –'

'No, no! Please don't accuse him' she interrupted. 'He is not so culpable as one might think. It is simply the misguided passion of a spoilt child. His mother and uncle have already forgiven him.'

'His mother, yes; but if I may say so, I don't believe his uncle is being quite so indulgent.'

'Be that as it may, monsieur, I shall try to imitate his mother. Little as I am experienced in these matters, it would appear that our will is impotent in affairs of the heart and can no more begin a passion than end it.'

'Alas, yes! That is only too true …'

A sigh completed Fabien's response, one which, skilfully timed, deliberately conveyed to the young woman a sense of personal agitation. Following this he continued, 'All the same, madame, regarding the present situation, I feel I must speak out and say what my feelings are. And in all honesty I cannot understand this blind passion of Maurice's for this woman. Please do not be offended by my frankness; but having seen and been with you, I fail to understand how he could prefer any other woman.'

'Monsieur!' Clotilde stammered, blushing and involuntarily moving away at this palpable avowal from Fabien.

'I will say no more if you insist,' he continued, 'only let me add this: Madame de Barthèle said just now that your marriage was a love match rather than one of convenience. In which case either she is wrong, or I ought to be astonished at seeing him ruining your happiness in this way. And then, surely, there can be no real love without jealousy. Do you not detest, are you not madly jealous of this woman who is about to invade your house, who has taken your husband from you?'

'That is as it may be, monsieur,' she returned. 'But the important thing at this moment is that Maurice is dangerously ill, and the doctor declares that only the presence of this woman can cure him.'

'True enough, perhaps,' Fabien replied, taking a delight in turning the knife in the young wife's wound, 'but supposing she can bring about his recovery, can she at the same time bring about his return to sanity? That is what concerns me most.'

'Monsieur, while I am grateful for your sympathy, I am not

a little surprised that you should take it on yourself to discuss my unhappy situation so warmly.'

'My warmth would not surprise you if you could read my heart; if you could appreciate the feelings which urge me on – feelings which are stronger even than those I have for my best friend.'

The avowal was so direct, so unmistakable, that Clotilde could not restrain a movement of alarm.

'Although I am listening to you,' she said, her breast rising and falling agitatedly, 'I fail to understand you.' And here she essayed to adopt a cold and reserved tone.

'Pardon me, pardon me!' Fabien went on, feigning an impassioned warmth, 'but I cannot help it. When I see my friend spurning your love, am I wrong if I ask you to reciprocate a friendly word, a smile, a gesture which could make me the happiest of men?'

There was no way she could mistake the meaning of his words. Pale and trembling she sprang from the divan. 'Pardon me, monsieur,' she said frigidly, 'but I think I can hear a carriage. It will probably be that of Madame Ducoudray, and I told Madame de Barthèle I would warn her of her arrival.' With these words she hurried out of the conservatory and disappeared from Fabien's view.

'Good!' he exclaimed as he carefully rearranged his collar and smoothed his cuffs. 'Things progress nicely. She ran away, which shows she was afraid to go on listening to me. Ah! they want me to play the rôle of assistant doctor, do they? Well and good! But they shall be made to pay me for my visits.'

Three

Three

La Rochefoucauld has declared in his cynical *Maxims* that there is always something in a friend's misfortunes which gives us a certain pleasure. La Rochefoucauld has put the maxim at its most philanthropic; he might equally well have stated that there is no misfortune which cannot be exploited, no catastrophe from which someone cannot take advantage, no calamity which some speculator cannot bend to his own profit. Thus Fabien de Rieulle and Léon de Vaux had seen in their friend Maurice de Barthèle's circumstances the opportunity to replace him; the first with his wife, the second with his mistress. Now that Léon de Vaux was no longer in any doubt that there had been a final break in the relationship between Maurice and Fernande a single simple question began to torment him, namely, who was to succeed or already had succeeded Maurice? This was a serious matter with him, for he was desperate to know the caprices of this woman who had accepted his society for so long without ever coming near to rewarding him. And now at last he saw, or thought he saw, the opportunity of replacing the former sovereign of her favours.

So, having brought her to the Barthèle country house, instead of taking her into the *salon* Léon led her into the garden under the pretext of showing off its beauties but in reality to put off the embarrassing explanations he foresaw coming. Enraptured at having Fernande to himself he had not even brought himself to the point of informing her of the real reason for this visit as Fabien had anticipated he would.

Instead he relied on the more audacious character of his friend to break the facts to her. But after showing her round the garden and pointing out to her the attractiveness of the place, he was finally forced to take her inside where, to the young woman's relief, they found Fabien waiting to greet them.

'Ah, Monsieur de Rieulle!' she cried: 'Here you are then at last! Really, I was beginning to wonder where you had disappeared to and what this mysterious excursion was all about! Monsieur de Vaux is being most evasive and enigmatic. But I am sure you will explain. What is this place? No one seems to be about. Could it be by any chance the palace of the Sleeping Beauty?'

'Just so, madame,' Fabien took her up, 'and you are the fairy who is to bring everything back to life.'

'A truce to this jesting!' Fernande returned with obvious displeasure. 'Come, tell me. Why are we here? Why are you looking so surprised? Don't you understand plain language? Enough! Tell me!'

'What!' Fabien exclaimed, completely taken aback. 'Hasn't that fool Léon told you?'

'My dear fellow,' Léon put in hastily with his usual fatuous dandyism, 'can't you understand that finding myself alone with madame I could do nothing but admire her and tell her for the hundredth time how much I adore her?'

'In which case you may consider me generous', Fernande rejoined, 'to have let you say it a hundred times without telling you I find it a hundred times too many.'

Normally good-natured, Fernande yet knew how to keep any semblance of over-familiarity at a distance and to stand on her dignity. This she did now, and her freezing look and icy tone put the young man firmly in his place. He tried to stammer out a few words of self-excuse. Fabien, who had no excuses to make, waited.

'Gentlemen,' Fernande continued still in her chilling tone, 'I have now seen this charming place which you tell me is for sale. Now what? If you are intending giving me a surprise, I warn you, I detest surprises.'

'Madame,' replied Léon endeavouring to assume an air of subtlety, 'you are at the home of someone we think you will be pleased to see again.'

'Ah! really?' returned Fernande hiding her anger under an ironical smile. 'I smell a trap here. Now, tell me at once: where am I?' As she posed the question she turned to Fabien with a frown that drew together her beautiful black eyebrows and continued, 'I speak to you, Monsieur de Rieulle, for I am sure you are too much of a gentleman to do me a bad turn or try out some stupid joke.'

Léon bit his lips, while Fabien, trying to smile, went on to confess, 'I won't hide the truth from you any longer, madame. Yes, this excursion has been arranged because it is urgent for you to be here. In a word it is because you are needed to give back life and hope to a sick person.'

'Indeed!' exclaimed Fernande still with an ironical expression and tone revealing a growing anger. 'You have taken it on yourselves to dispose of me in a strange fashion, I must say! I do not recall having given you the right – But unless I am mistaken,' she interrupted herself, 'our solitude is about to be broken.'

In fact at that moment the door of the *salon* was opened, and Madame de Barthèle, warned by Clotilde of her arrival, entered. On the entrance of the baroness a noticeable change came over the courtesan, who drew herself up to her full height and assumed a stance of cold reserve. The attitude of Madame de Barthèle was one of artificial composure. A factitious smile momentarily displaced her normal look of open, naive kindliness, and her curtsey of greeting was too exaggerated to be polite. Nevertheless, on raising her eyes and examining Fernande with that infallible glance with which one woman can size up another, and noting the exquisite taste of her costume and the severe beauty of her face and figure, she at once assumed a more natural expression and hastened to counteract her first reaction by saying warmly, 'I thank you, madame, for the time you have so kindly accorded to us in consenting to bring back happiness to our family.'

Fernande, no less astonished by the baroness's words, but recognising in her a woman of high society and breeding, returned her greeting with equal civility: 'When I know how I can be of service to you, madame –' she began.

'Of service!' the baroness interjected, beginning to feel an unexpected sympathy with the stranger. 'Far more than that indeed. The doctor will tell you.'

Fernande gave an expressive glance towards Fabien and Léon as if to demand the reason for these words of the baroness which to her came as a complete enigma.

'Madame,' Léon hurriedly replied in response to this mute appeal and indicating Madame de Barthèle with respect, 'here is a mother who is looking to you to restore her son to health.'

At this explanation, given in a slightly mocking tone, Fernande began to sense a vague presentiment that this adventure, begun so lightly, was to become something serious, perhaps even to end in deep misfortune. She therefore begged Madame de Barthèle to explain herself. Whereupon the latter, forgetting her original intention to play the *grande dame*, and succumbing to Fernande's charm, replied in her usual impulsive way: 'But you must understand the desperate situation, madame. The poor boy loves you so much! And his passion for you has thrown him into a dreadful state of apathy, so that he no longer has any wish to go on living.'

Fernande's astonishment manifested itself by a gesture of indignation so expressive that the baroness saw at once that she had cruelly wounded the feelings of the young woman. Seizing her hand impulsively she went on 'Ah, madame! I beg you not to be offended. Be kind and forgiving, and make up for the grief you have inflicted no doubt unknowingly, and rest assured of our eternal gratitude.'

But at her words Fernande became dreadfully pale. Seeing her emotion, and comprehending how her words, taken in a certain sense, must have been felt as insulting, the baroness broke off and began to utter broken apologies. Her embarrassment was increased by hearing Léon remark in an aside to Fernande, as if to take revenge for the snub she had administered to him, 'And now you know what it is all about.' Both women felt the impact of his insensitive observation.

Turning to the baroness Fernande observed frigidly, 'I no longer seek an explanation from you, madame, but from these gentlemen who invited me here in the first place. Now perhaps, messieurs, you will have the goodness to give me the full explanation of all this.'

Madame de Barthèle, alarmed at the way in which the scene threatened to terminate, tried to put in words in defence of the young men; but Fernande, realising she was the controlling figure in the situation, interrupted her with, 'Not a word more, madame, if you please. I see clearly that you are one of those beings blessed by fortune with wealth, good society, virtue, everything in fact. What can there possibly be in common beween you and such as I? We have been brought together by a plot concocted by these two – shall I say gentlemen? And as proof to you that I have had no hand in it I beg leave to go.' And with these words, after a ceremonious curtsey to the baroness but without so much as a glance at Fabien and Léon, she turned and took several steps towards the door. Only then did Madame de Barthèle recover from this unexpected dénouement and rush across to place herself between the door and Fernande. 'But madame, madame!' she cried piteously. 'Pray don't leave us like this! Have pity on a mother! My son is ill. It is for him I beg you to stay.'

Whatever Fernande's response might have been was forestalled by the sudden appearance of Clotilde in the doorway.

'Ah, my dear!' exclaimed Madame de Barthèle going up to her and seizing her hands, 'Help me to persuade madame to stay and save your husband!'

Fernande remained fixed to the spot with astonishment, and the two young women exchanged looks impossible to describe. Brief as it was, this interchange between the wife and the mistress was enough to make each understand the nature of their rivalry: on the one hand the glamour of the unknown and unexperienced, of notoriety, glitter, passion; on the other innocence, purity, moral right, beauty accepted and familiar. A slight bow passed between them.

'My dear,' Madame de Barthèle hastened to explain, 'this is Madame Ducoudray.'

'Madame Ducoudray!' exclaimed Fernande in astonishment, perceiving herself indicated under that name.

'Yes, madame,' Fabien hastened to explain. 'We thought it better from the social aspect to bring you under a name which wouldn't compromise you. Pardon us if we have been indiscreet.'

For the courtesan this was the final indignity. After throwing at Fabien the look of a lioness at bay, turning to the baroness she said, 'Madame, I too have my pride. If you receive me it must be for myself. To do so under a false name would be a dishonour and humiliation for both of us. I must tell you: I am not married; I am not called Madame Ducoudray; my name is Fernande.'

'Under whatever name,' Madame de Barthèle returned imploringly, 'please believe me you are welcome. It is we who suggested you should come, and who beg you to stay and save my son.'

At this point yet a fresh turn was given to the scene by the entrance of Monsieur de Montgiroux. On seeing Fernande he stopped short and uttered a stifled exclamation. His sudden and unexpected appearance, his exclamation and his look of incredulity had their effect on the different persons in the room. 'There is the answer to your question,' Fabien remarked in an aside to his friend. 'The count is the reigning prince!'

What can there be between the count and this woman? Madame de Barthèle asked herself.

Is this a revenge on the part of Léon de Vaux? Fernande wondered.

'*Mon Dieu*! So it is Fernande Maurice is in love with!' the count muttered.

Clotilde alone, calm amid the storm of emotions around her, appeared unaffected and was the first to speak. 'Has the doctor sent you to tell us anything, Uncle?' she asked.

'Yes, yes!' he replied eagerly, only too pleased to return to fact and reality. 'He knows of madame's arrival and is awaiting her impatiently.'

'You hear, madame?' the baroness addressed Fernande beseechingly.

'Since it appears I have this mysterious power, madame,' Fernande said relenting, 'I put myself in your hands.'

'Mysterious power indeed!' said the count in an injured tone. 'It seems my niece's husband, poor fool, has had the misfortune to know you and fall violently in love with you – like so many others, it seems.'

The count spoke with such an accent of displeasure that Clotilde imagined he intended a moral lesson for the courtesan. 'Oh, Uncle!' she cried, throwing herself into his arms, 'Not now, please!'

But the peer was too upset to leave things as they were, and in answer to Fernande's expression of hope that the invalid's condition was being exaggerated rejoined bitterly, 'My dear madame, he is delirious, and in his delirium he keeps calling out your name; accuses you of ingratitude, coldness, infidelity, perfidy, treason and heaven knows what else.'

The scene, through the count's imprudence, threatened to degenerate into a personal quarrel between himself and Fernande; seeing which the baroness proceeded to turn on him indignantly.

'Monsieur le comte,' she rebuked him, 'you seem to forget that Madame Ducoudray is here as my guest, and that of my niece, and is in my son's house. This is hardly the time to begin moral strictures or to seek for such explanation as you apparently wish to have from her.'

'Yes, yes, Uncle!' Clotilde appealed without understanding

the violent emotion he was experiencing. 'Let us think only of Maurice.'

'Of Maurice?' exclaimed Fernande. 'Is the invalid called Maurice?'

'Yes, madame,' the baroness confirmed. 'Did you not know whose house you were in? I am the Baroness de Barthèle.'

'Maurice de Barthèle!' cried Fernande in a voice of agonised incredulity. 'Oh, *mon Dieu, mon Dieu*!' As she uttered the words she placed her hands over her face, and after swaying blindly fell half unconscious into the arms of Clotilde and the baroness who had hurried to her assistance.

On regaining her senses and finding herself the object of the attentions of Maurice's mother and wife, Fernande, by a supreme effort of will, imposed a forced control over her emotion and thanked the two women. Once they saw that she had recovered, they sent word to the three men that they could come back into the room. Once there they waited with some impatience to be taken to Maurice's room, sensing that the real drama was to be played out there. But unknown to them, for Fernande, that had already been enacted in her heart.

'Madame,' she addressed Clotilde, 'it is you who must take me to Maurice's bedside. I will not appear before him unless presented by you and his mother.'

It needed all her courage to enable herself to be seen by Maurice between these two, for she had loved him with all the strength of a first veritable love: a love which had been the lodestar of her life, making it possible for her to put behind her the hectic, factitious existence she had come to adopt against all the instincts and tenets of her upbringing.

* * *

She had first met Maurice de Barthèle at the famous Chantilly races, where he had entered two of his horses, one of which he rode himself. Neither his wife nor his mother had accompanied him; so it was that he found himself on his own among his former bachelor friends and associates, notably Fabien de Rieulle and Léon de Vaux. Like Maurice, Fabien had two horses running, and thus their old rivalry was being resumed. And as usual Maurice was the victor with two firsts, with Fabien having to try to console himself with two seconds.

Fernande had never met Maurice. She had only just begun to make a noise in the demi-mondaine world of Paris when Maurice had married and more or less given up his old haunts and bachelor freedom. The races over, everyone dispersed to their various destinations. Finding him on his own, Fabien and Léon began telling him of the delightful suppers and entertainment to be had at Fernande's and offered to take him to her house. After some demur Maurice had let himself be persuaded, stipulating only that no word of his visit should be mentioned in case it came to the ears of his family. It was in this way that Maurice was presented to Fernande for the first time.

To begin with Fernande took notice of Maurice merely as the winner of the most important race of the day and as one more visitor among the many who paid court to her; and she behaved in the manner expected of her: that is to say she was coquettish, frank, gay, laughing and making the others laugh at her witty and sometimes free comments. But as the evening wore on she observed that Maurice, while watching her closely, remained serious, scarcely even smiling at the *badinage* that went on round him; that he spoke only now and then, but when he did it was to make a serious observation rather than to utter frivolities. This, together with the vibrant tone of his voice and his handsome face with its dark expressive eyes, made the courtesan regard him with particular attention; and as the evening progressed she felt in spite of herself instinctively attracted to him, sensing in him with a woman's perception something deeper than was to be found in the rest of the *bon vivants*. She observed too that whenever the conversation became – at least when judged by respectable society – too libertine, an air of sadness came over him as though he were saying to himself, What a pity! So young, so beautiful, and yet so loose! Yet despite such sentiments Maurice became gradually aware that something about the looks and personality of the courtesan struck a vibrant chord in him. She was different, he felt, from the rest of the *bon vivants* there. So that when finally the party broke up at three in the morning, he returned home with one memory in his mind – that of Fernande; unknowing that she, too, after the noisy company had left, in the silence of her solitude, was thinking of him. Each recalled the looks, gestures and words of the other and fell asleep, secretly hoping they might meet again.

In effect, on the afternoon of the next day Maurice called on her just as she was going out. Both betrayed by their blushes and constraint that each had been thinking of the other and wishing for a second meeting. Nevertheless, as if both too felt the need to prepare themselves for the encounter, Maurice insisted that Fernande should not put off her intention of going out on his account, while she for her part declared she was only making a short visit and would return in a few minutes, and enjoined him to go in, make himself at home and wait for her.

Left alone in the apartments of this woman *à la mode* whom he had met quite by chance but who nevertheless now took up all his thoughts, Maurice found himself torn by hitherto unknown emotions – emotions double-faced in that they were caused in part by a sense of elation at being caught up in new unsuspected sensations of conquest and adventure, and in part from feelings of guilt forewarning him he was about to enter into an immoral and guilty association.

However that might be, he was devoured by a curiosity to penetrate the mystery he felt behind this woman who was beginning to have such a powerful hold on him. He looked round him with a curious eye. The *salon*, in which he was, instead of being furnished in the usual gaudy taste of such women and cluttered with bric-à-brac, revealed a fastidious, almost severe taste. On the walls were paintings of the great masters of early times. A piano stood in the centre of the room, its top covered with music scores, and not far from it a table littered with books and albums. A half-opened door caught his eye. Looking in, he found it to consist of an artist's studio, with statues, busts, canvases and easels scattered pell-mell in typical artist fashion. An unfinished canvas on an easel faced him. On the other side of the room another half-opened door revealed on brief inspection a bedroom. Maurice turned away with a strange and violent contraction of the heart. He then turned his attention to the various scores littering the piano, and found them to consist mainly of operas by Weber, Rossini and Hérold. He passed on in astonishment to the table and picked up some of the books. These included volumes of Molière, Bossuet and Corneille. Nothing in the place suggested the home of a courtesan – rather that of some cultured duchess of the faubourg Saint-Germain.

As he stood wondering, Fernande returned. There might well have been a measure of calculation on the part of the young woman in leaving Maurice alone in her apartment for that short time: perhaps an instinctive feeling that a certain moral establishment between them was essential before a resumption of their association. So, comprehending his feelings as much by her instinct as by the look of astonishment on his face, she took it on herself to be the first to broach the all-important subject of their future relationship by putting him to the test.

'I would wager, monsieur,' she began brusquely and looking at him with a piercing glance, 'that you thought you had only to call on me to be accepted without question. Oh, there is no need for excuses,' she continued, cutting short his stammered protestations. 'I have long lost the right to be offended. You have only seen me once, but no doubt my reputation has gone before me.'

As she spoke her voice lost its attempted coldness to

become charged with sadness. Maurice thought he even glimpsed the suspicion of a tear.

'Madame,' he replied, no less moved than she, 'my sincerity must be my excuse. The impression you made on me last night has haunted me, and ever since I have had only one desire – to see you again.'

Fernande smiled, seated herself on a divan and made a sign to Maurice to come and sit beside her. 'Thank you for your words,' she said. 'I feel I can believe them. And in return I will be equally frank with you. Honestly and truly, if ever I would like to please anyone it is you.'

'*Grand Dieu!*' Maurice exclaimed, carried away by his emotion. 'Can you really mean that?'

'Now listen to me,' she said, imposing silence on the young man with a gesture full of charm and grace. He obeyed with a look of doubt and passion there was no mistaking. Fernande continued, 'Before we come to an agreement I want to put all my cards on the table so that you will be under no delusion about me. I must tell you I am independent of all and any favours. I am complete mistress of my heart and person. From a man who says he loves me, then, I have need of nothing but his love. Only on your acceptance of these facts will I accept you. Happiness for happiness. Yes, I love you.'

At these last words Fernande's voice failed her, and the trembling hand she put out towards him fell back on her lap. Most men would have thrown themselves at her feet, kissed that hand and tried to convince her of their good faith by repeated vows. Maurice rose.

'Now listen to me,' he asserted. 'On the honour of a gentleman I love you as I have never loved any woman. And so, forget my hundred thousand pounds revenue and think of me as having nothing but myself to offer. Only, dispose of me as you will.' Then going on his knees before her: 'Do you believe my word?' he demanded. 'Do you believe in my love?'

'Oh yes, yes!' she cried, deeply moved and interlacing her beautiful arms round his neck. 'You are no Fabien, that I know!'

The lips of the young lovers met in a long impassioned kiss. Then as Maurice became more pressing she went on, 'Listen, Maurice. I have shamelessly reversed all the proprieties. I was the first to say I love you. Well, be it that way. Leave all the initiatives to me.'

Maurice stood up and looked down on her with a look of unutterable love. 'You are my queen, my soul, my life,' he murmured. 'Command, and I obey.'

'Well and good, dearest. But let us talk. We must come to know each other beyond all doubt. I am only Fernande, a poor girl who has made herself rich, whom the respectable address as 'madame' but at the same time put beyond the pale of their society. A courtesan, in short.'

'Fernande!' he exclaimed, his heart contracting at her cruel words. 'Don't talk so, please!'

'On the contrary, my love, you must accustom yourself to what the world will say to you about me. Don't expect them to be tactful. In any case, why should I complain? I am in no position to act the martyr. All the same, without going into the past, let me tell you it was not I who made myself into what I have become.' Her words ended in a heavy sigh. Before he could speak she pursued, 'And now you know all you need to know about me, at least for the moment. Be generous then, my dear, and if you really love me, pity rather than blame me. I know you found me among a crowd of worthless associates, but that is one of the penalties of my past way of life. Yet even there I felt drawn towards you as if by some strange presentiment. I can't help it. I can find no balm to my poor heart except in a true devotion. To be able to give and receive real love! – oh, that would be to redeem the past. To redeem myself! Can you understand that, Maurice? Oh, say you understand me!' A look clouded with involuntary tears accompanied her question.

'Oh yes!' he replied. 'I do! I do!'

'I believe you!' she said, her tearfulness giving way to happiness at his heartfelt words. 'But I can scarcely credit it. I had come to the point of telling myself I should never find love, real disinterested love. To fight against this I have devoted myself desperately to the things I had some gift for in my young days at Saint-Denis and just after – art, music and books.'

Had Maurice not been so newly and deeply in love he would no doubt have been asking himself if this was a courtesan speaking. But, typically male and absorbed in his desires, he could only gaze at her in a rapture of adoration. 'How beautiful you are!' he cried, 'and how I adore you!' As he spoke he drew her to him. She read and understood the desire in his eyes. Responding with a brief kiss, but freeing herself, she said with a radiant smile, 'Now that I know you love me, come with me.' And taking him by the hand she led him to a door hidden by a damask curtain and which had escaped his notice during his recent cursory examination of the room.

'What is this? A surprise?' he asked as he followed her, wondering.

'Yes,' she replied with a meaning smile. She opened the door, revealing to him a charming boudoir all in white. White muslin curtains hung at the casement window; white curtains draped and half concealed a bed.

'Oh, Fernande!' he exclaimed as he devoured her with his eyes. 'Where have you brought me?'

'Where no man has ever been before. I have always kept this little room for the man I loved, if ever I did love.'

With these words she drew him inside and closed the door behind them.

* * *

From this time on Fernande organised her existence afresh and in accordance with her long-cherished wishes. The realisation of an affection that was sincere seemed to give her a new life and efface the shame of the past. Her new-found happiness gave her not only a yet more striking beauty but a radiation of joy and well-being which made her even more attractive. But her former admirers complained when she was no longer to be seen in her old haunts and no longer favoured them with her celebrated parties. She let them murmur. Happy to be alone with Maurice time went by all too rapidly; and on his part he loved only those too brief hours spent with his adored mistress. Yet unlike her he could not enjoy the same degree of carefree happiness, placed as he was between Clotilde, whose existence he carefully hid from Fernande, and Fernande whose existence he carefully hid from his wife and tried to hide from the prying eyes of the world; and having to feign a tenderness for his wife which he did not feel and to his mistress a freedom he did not really have, his guilty conscience denied him the peace of mind and happiness she was experiencing. In short, Fernande was able to give herself to him utterly, whereas he could only reciprocate in part.

This situation continued for several months.

But nothing in life lasts. The storm broke over the lovers' heads for the very reasons they had taken to prevent it. Fernande was not one of those women who can disappear from the world without the fact being noticed. To isolate herself, to break with her former existence in a burst of repentance might possibly be accepted, but not for the sake of a new lover. She had been watched, spied on by jealous would-be suitors. Maurice had been seen entering her door and coming out hours later, and at times when everyone else had been refused.

So it was that one morning Fernande received one of those letters in a disguised hand against which there is no legal redress and no hope of rejoinder, but which wound and even destroy as surely as steel or poison. It was an anonymous letter which ran:

> Madame – A noble family has been plunged into despair because of your liaison with Baron Maurice de Barthèle. Be as generous as you are beautiful, and return a son to his mother and *a husband to his wife*.

Fernande had just risen from a night of golden sleep

customary with her since her fulfilled love for Maurice. The blow was terrible in its effect, the facts it revealed shattering. A second reading of the letter, for the first had been too much of a blow for her to take in, only confirmed the first. Yet she still doubted. Could it be possible that Maurice had kept such a secret from her? Had she to believe that each time he left her, her who loved him with all the strength of her being, it was to return to his wife? ... Maurice, then, was no better than any of the other men.

To one of Fernande's ardent and frank nature all doubt was intolerable. To end it she determined then and there to discover the truth, however bitter. Among her female friends was a woman who called herself a *femme de lettres* from the fact that she occasionally wrote a poor novel or an indifferent play. Madame d'Aulnay, besides, was one of those busybodies who know everyone and everything. Snatching up pen and paper she dashed down:

> Dear Madame d'Aulnay – I have been asked for the address of Mme. Maurice de Barthèle, but I do not know it. I am sure, however, that you will be able to give it me. Can you tell me at the same time something about her? For example, is she young and attractive?
> As always your devoted and grateful
> Fernande

After giving the sealed note to her *valet de chambre* with orders to deliver it to Madame d'Aulnay and to bring back her answer, Fernande waited in an agony of suspense. Some twenty minutes later the valet returned. She took the perfumed envelope from him with a shaking hand, knowing it contained her life or death. After a moment's agonising hesitation she tore it open and as through a mist read:

> *Chère belle,*
> Madame la Baronne de Barthèle lives with her mother-in-law at her hotel, rue de Varennes no.24. While between women, you know, such compliments are not usually or easily paid, I have to admit that she is a charming young person.

But now for yourself. What has happened to you of late, my dear? No one sees anything of you nowadays. All the same, you know you are always welcome at rue de Provence, no.11.

Armandine d'Aulnay

There could no longer be any doubt: Maurice was married and had a young and charming wife.

It was eleven o'clock. Maurice would be along as usual at mid-day. Maurice! Another woman's husband! Fernande's first reaction was to break into a storm of sobbing; but as time wore on her tears began to give way to a growing anger, so that it felt to her as though the last drops were of fire and burned her eyelids. At last, as the clock struck twelve, she heard a carriage stop at her door, then a ring, followed in turn by Maurice's well-known footsteps in the ante-room. A moment later the door opened and he entered, his face expressing all the happiness he felt at being with her.

From the chair in which she was sitting, Fernande, pale and motionless, watched him approach with a fixed and lifeless look, Madame d'Aulnay's note clenched in her hands. In his haste to greet her he did not at first observe her expression, and bending over her prepared to give her his usual kiss of greeting. At this presumption a sudden blush replaced the pallor of her face, and pushing him away she got up and stepped abruptly away from him.

'Monsieur,' she said in a dull and trembling voice, 'you have lied to me like any common menial!'

Maurice stood motionless and wordless as though stunned; then, taken aback by her unnatural looks, he made a step towards her, asking what had come over her.

'Monsieur,' she silenced him, 'you are a liar! A common deceiver! You are deceiving two of us – me and your wife. You are married. You see, I have found you out.'

He uttered a despairing cry, feeling the unutterable happiness of his liaison slipping away from him. As stricken as she he could only bow his head and fall without a word into a chair.

–55–

'So you see,' she went on pitilessly, 'honour calls on you to go back to your wife, and on me never to receive you here again.' And passing into the bedroom she put on a coat and the first hat she could lay hands on, and going out told her servant to inform Monsieur de Barthèle that she would not be back that day.

Walking haphazardly, Fernande eventually found herself in the rue de Provence. Not knowing where else to go she mechanically went up to number 11, rang the bell and went in.

'Ah! So it is really you, my angel!' Madame d'Aulnay cried. 'What a surprise! I see you have felt the reproach I made you in my little note. What have you been doing with yourself all the winter? But what is the matter with you, *chère petite*? You are pale as a sheet. Tell me ...'

'I am ... oh, I am the unhappiest woman in the world,' Fernande managed to get out through a sudden attack of sobs.

'You, unhappy, with all your youth and beauty? Impossible, my dear! Now, if only you can tell me I am certain I can –'

'Oh, don't ask me to explain. I don't know where to begin. I am dreadfully unhappy, that is all.'

'I know, I know, my dear! Some grand passion, I'll be bound! Surely you are not so foolish as to give way to anything like that at your age. That would be stupid.'

'Yes, yes, you are right,' Fernande answered without having listened to a word the literary lady had said.

'Right? I should think so! Now then,' Madame D'Aulnay continued, drying Fernande's eyes with her handkerchief and making her sit beside her, 'dry those tears which only spoil your beautiful looks, and listen to me. You know the proverb: A lover lost means ten gained. That should be easy enough with you. Now listen. Spend the day with me. We will go out and find distraction, eh? What do you say?' Fernande could only reply with a murmured mechanical, 'Yes.'

'Good! We will take a drive to the Bois. The weather is perfect for it. Agreed, then?'

Taking silence for consent Madame d'Aulnay took Fernande's arm with the intention of conducting her to the door. But the *femme de lettres* had quite a following of friends, social and literary, who were in the habit of calling on her. So it was that at that moment her servant announced a visitor, which proved to be the Comte de Montgiroux. On his entrance Fernande rose hastily as though to escape, but Madame d'Aulnay prevented her with: 'No, stay, my dear. Monsieur de Montgiroux is a charming man.'

The count recognised Fernande, whom he knew by sight and who he had been told was noted for her wit, charm and elegance. He therefore approached her with the old-world courtesy of the last century replaced by us nowadays with the less formal English handshake. Madame d'Aulnay was quick to perceive the impression made by Fernande on the count, and as the peer was one of those whom she counted among her admirers, she gave him a particularly warm welcome, adding, 'Would you be content to join us later for dinner, Count?'

'That goes without saying, dear madame,' he rejoined with an expressive glance at Fernande and a bow to each of the ladies, 'but only on condition that you permit me to order the meal.'

'You know you are perfectly free here to do as you please. So do so, my dear Count.'

After more polite conversation Monsieur de Montgiroux took his leave; and ten minutes later each of the ladies received a magnificent bouquet from the most élite and expensive florist in all Paris.

'Well, my sweet,' Madame d'Aulnay demanded as they began their drive, 'what do you think of him?'

'Think of whom?' Fernande said, her thoughts a thousand miles away.

'Our dinner guest, of course.'

'I'm afraid I didn't take much notice of him.'

'Not notice him? But you can take it from me he is altogether a charming gentleman,' Madame d'Aulnay protested, beginning to pursue a plan she had been meditating as regards Fernande. 'And what is more, I will wager you have already made a deep impression on him.'

Fernande's only response was a sad smile, having scarcely taken in the implication of her friend's words. Lost in her own thoughts, she was beginning to ask herself whether she had not, in the shock of Maurice's deceit, been too severe, and, if he were to appear suddenly before her to ask her forgiveness she would not weaken and relent. But then, realising that this could never be, she made an attempt to pull herself together, telling herself that, after all, she was only what the world had made of her and called her, namely, a courtesan, a kept woman, and known to all as such. So it was that, on their return to Madame d'Aulnay's they found the table laid and everything prepared. At six o'clock prompt the count arrived. At dinner, placed between them, he chatted with his aristocratic politeness equally with both. Fernande, whose innate good taste enabled her to appreciate such qualities in others, felt bound to acknowledge that her friend's eulogy of the count was in no way exaggerated, and once or twice she even went so far as to respond to his carefully timed advances with an appreciative smile.

The meal over, their hostess announced that to her great regret she had a brief visit to pay to the director of the theatre which was putting on her latest play. Fernande, uncertain whether Madame d'Aulnay's excuse was genuine or a fabrication in order to leave her alone with the count, felt a constriction of the heart. Was she really being treated with such contrived levity? But then, returning to her former severe reflection, she asked herself why not. Wasn't she, to them, just a courtesan?

Reasoning in this manner she forced herself to look with factitious gaiety at the count.

'Madame,' he began, encouraged by her more friendly manner and bringing his chair closer to the sofa on which she was half reclining, 'I have never had the honour of meeting you previously, but I have more than once heard you spoken of with admiration, and I can well understand how it is that people declare it is impossible to know you without falling in love with you.'

'Thank you for the compliment, monsieur le comte,' she replied with a smile which hid her feelings. 'You must surely be aware that I am one of those women to whom one can say anything.'

'No, no, madame,' he protested. 'Perhaps I did come here in that belief. But now I have met you I have come to know your true worth. And I only ask that you would be willing to give me some of your time on occasions when my duties as a minister leave me free to see you.'

'Really, monsieur le comte, you are a charming man,' she said still with her sad smile and quite taken by his courteous declaration of intent, 'and it is quite impossible to resist you!' She gave him her hand and he covered it with rapturous kisses.

Soon afterwards Madame d'Aulnay returned, and after a short while the count had the delicacy to take his leave. Fernande soon followed. But on reaching home she found the count's *valet de chambre* awaiting her, a missive in his hand. Taking it into the *salon* she opened it and read:

> When one has had the pleasure of meeting you, and when one is dying with desire to meet you again, at what time may one hope for admittance to your door?
>
> > Comte de Montgiroux

Taking up a pen Fernande wrote:

> Any day until mid-day; any day until three when it rains; any evening when I am entertaining; any night when one wishes to make love.
>
> > Fernande

Poor Fernande! She must indeed have been suffering to be able to pen such a charming *billet-doux*.

As from that day Fernande's existence changed completely, returning to its former round of noise, movement, excitement, entertainment, spectacles – all and anything in an effort to kill the pain at her heart, the memories of her mind: in a word, to escape from her thoughts. The Comte de Montgiroux, whose assiduous attentions were additional incentive, seeing this became more and more jealous; for while Fernande had never deceived any of her previous lovers, she had always insisted, as she had done with Maurice, that she must be independent, and they had no option but to accept her terms or lose her. But the poor count, while agreeing to her demand, plagued as he was on the one hand by the proprietorial questionings of his old flame Madame de Barthèle, and on the other held back by his social and political status, in the nature of things was prevented from accompanying the courtesan in all her febrile pleasures and was constantly tormented by pangs of jealousy – a jealousy augmented by his awareness of his age of sixty as against hers of twenty-two, and by imagining she was deceiving him for some younger man.

Among these were two of her most ardent pursuers, Fabien de Rieulle and Léon de Vaux, the difference between them being that while the first took on the air of a conquering lover, the second sought to win her by the persistent attentions of a humble would-be wooer. Fernande saw clearly into their respective characters and worth – Fabien, a calculating experienced seducer, Léon, a feather-brained dandy – and succumbed to neither. And in fact both men were coming to realise that she was a changed woman, at times scarcely bothering to listen to their compliments and protestations, or, if she did, only to retort with bitter sarcasms; and in fact from being normally kind and responsive, became more and more embittered and caustic.

'My sweet angel,' Madame d'Aulnay remarked to her one day in the course of a rare visit, 'what has come over you of late? You are no longer the same woman. You are really becoming quite unsupportable. I no longer seem to know you.'

'Eh, madame!' Fernande rejoined, 'who can say they ever really knew me?'

'I must warn you, *chère petite*, you will make a lot of enemies if you go on like this.'

'That at any rate will enable me to find out who my real friends are.' At the end of the visit the *femme de lettres* had left with a flea in her ear and a rift between them.

It was soon after this incident that Fabien and Léon had come to her to propose a jaunt out to Fontenay-aux-Roses where, they said, a charming villa was for sale which they thought might take her fancy. As this was something new and different it suited Fernande to agree to their proposal. We have already seen what transpired at this villa and what the real purpose of the visit was on that fateful day; how she had been accepted by Madame de Barthèle; how she and the Comte de Montgiroux had recognised each other; how, finally, after being overwhelmed by the knowledge that she was in the home of her former lover, by sheer strength of character she had come to take control of the unexpected and almost incredible situation. And it was with pangs of heartache that the realisation came to her that it was being left to her, the despised courtesan, to restore her ailing lover to health and bring peace of mind to his family.

Such were her thoughts as she followed Madame de Barthèle and Clotilde up the stairs to Maurice's bedroom.

Four

Four

As we have already intimated there were two doors leading into Maurice's room: one in the corridor, the other a private one by the bedhead. It had been behind this latter that the two women had overheard the conversation between Maurice and his two friends the previous evening.

The little troupe stopped outside the door in the passage.

'Please take care, madame,' the baroness said pointing the door out to Fernande, 'the doctor has warned us about possible harmful reactions. But I leave everything in your hands. All I ask from you is the cure of my son.' Clotilde said nothing, but her look conveyed her corroboration of her mother-in-law's words. The courtesan looked from one to the other with an involuntary pang, fully appreciating the maternal love of the one and the touching resignation of the other. With a sign of understanding she quietly opened the door. But on the threshold a mist came over her eyes and she was forced to pause and recover herself. While doing so she heard Maurice's voice cry out despairingly, 'Leave me! Leave me! Only let me see her once more before I die!'

Cut to the quick the three women hurried into the room, Clotilde and Madame de Barthèle taking up their position on either side of the bed, Fernande at the foot. A strange unnatural silence ensued. The light in the room was dimmed by the drawn curtains, but Fernande could make out Maurice half sitting in bed, staring at each of them in turn with an expression of stupor. Then, as though unbelieving of what he imagined he saw, and feeling his strength overtaxed by the effort, he fell back on the pillow, inert. His wife and mother were on the point of rushing to him when Doctor Gaston stopped them with an imperious gesture. Fernande understood that her moment had come. A piano stood in a recess between the two windows. Seating herself at it she began to play softly the prelude to the 'Ombra adorata' from Gounod's *Romeo and Juliet*, one of Maurice's favourite arias and one which she had sung for him so many times during their brief liaison. As she sang the aria her exquisite voice filled the room as if with magic, and all in it, as though entranced, seemed to suspend their breath. Fernande finished the aria in an atmosphere of almost religious silence. Sensing the effect she had produced, she felt she dared to show herself to the invalid, and slowly approached the bed. At the same time the doctor drew back one of the curtains. To Maurice it seemed as if an apparition had materialised before him.

'Maurice,' she said softly as she held out her hand to him, 'I have come to see you.'

At these, her first words, the young man's first movement was to turn to his wife and mother as if to ask them if this incredible visitation was with their knowledge and consent. Seeing them standing there in smiling acceptance, in a spontaneous reaction of guilt and self-reproach he covered his face with his hands and fell back on to the pillow, overcome. Fernande saw it was up to her now to explain everything to her lover. She took hold of his hand and trying to be indifferent to the shudder which the mere touch sent through him: 'Maurice,' she began, 'I have come at the request of your wife and mother to tell you that for their sake, and mine, you must get better.' Then as he tried to speak she went on hurriedly, 'Listen to me, Maurice. It is for me to speak and justify myself. Do you suppose I have acted as I have towards you out of caprice? that I have been living calmly with no regrets, no remorse? that I have been happy losing you? haven't suffered horribly? Think of all three of us, Maurice – two women whose lives revolve round you, while the third would die of remorse if you died, then say if you have the right to want to die.'

While Fernande was speaking the invalid, by a new-found expression in his eyes, by his breathing which seemed to come with greater strength, seemed to those watching him to show an unhoped-for semblance of life. A smile, even, came to his lips which, though a melancholy one, was the first to be seen for so long a time. He tried to reply to her, but emotion rather than weakness prevented him. The doctor, delighted by these symptoms, motioned to the three women to go warily.

'Dear Maurice,' his mother said, taking the doctor's cue, 'both Clotilde and I know everything. There is no need for you to feel ashamed. We understand.'

'Yes, Maurice,' Clotilde said in support of his mother. 'We understand.' Fernande said nothing, only giving way to a profound sigh. Maurice, too overwhelmed to be able to put his thoughts in order, could only gaze in astonishment at the three women. The doctor had closely observed the reaction of the persons involved, especially that of the invalid, and proceeded to take control.

'Now then, ladies,' he said, intervening with respectful authority, 'we mustn't tire our patient. Rest is what he needs most of all. Let us leave him for a while, then after dinner we might entertain him with a little music.' Here, seeing a look of alarm appear on Maurice's face and interpreting it he went on, addressing the baroness while indicating Fernande, 'Perhaps Madame la Baronne will be good enough to show our visitor to her room.'

'What!' Maurice exclaimed, unable to restrain his relief and joy. 'Is Fernande staying, then?'

'Yes,' Gaston replied casually. 'Madame is going to spend a day or two with us.'

A delighted smile lit up Maurice's face, while the doctor pursued, 'Well now, since I have been accepted as dictator here, you must all obey my injunctions. Besides, I am not prescribing undesirable things. All I ask is a couple of hours rest and quiet for Maurice.' Holding out a draught he had prepared to Fernande: 'Here, madame,' he said, 'give this to the patient, tell him he must not torment himself, and if he doesn't obey our orders you will scold him severely.'

Fernande took the potion and offered it to Maurice without a word; but her smile was so ingratiating, her look so imploring that, after being in rebellion for so long against all orders, he took it meekly, and after drinking it lay down blissfully rocked by the thought that she would still be there when he awoke. Seeing this, the three women tiptoed from the room.

'It is so very kind of you, madame,' the baroness said to Fernande as soon as they were outside. 'Now you understand, I hope, why, having gone so far, I beg you will continue your kindness by staying with us for a few days. I know it will mean a sacrifice on your part to be away from Paris and its pleasures, but we will do our best to make up for it.'

'And I join my request to that of Madame de Barthèle,' Clotilde added.

'I am at your orders,' Fernande replied simply.

'Thank you, madame,' Clotilde said, and with a reaction of silent gratitude took Fernande's hand in hers, only to start back in some alarm.

'Oh, *mon Dieu*!' she cried. 'Are you feeling well? Your hand is like ice.'

'Take no notice,' Fernande hurriedly reassured her. 'I shall be better when I have had time to recover from my emotions. I beg your pardon for it.'

'But it is only to be expected you should feel as you do,' said Madame de Barthèle with your usual goodness of heart and thoughtlessness of tongue. 'The poor boy loves you so much, and quite naturally you feel the same for him. One has only to see you to understand that.' Then she stopped short, aware too late that her words could only hurt her daughter-in-law and intensify the feelings of her visitor.

* * *

While the scene in Maurice's bedroom was being concluded, another of a very different kind was being played in the *salon* between Monsieur de Montgiroux and the two young men.

The peer had learned from Madame d'Aulnay that Fabien and Léon were two of the most assiduous admirers of his beautiful young mistress who, hiding nothing for the simple reason that she had nothing to hide, received and went about with them freely, so intensifying his doubts and suspicions. By conversing with them the count reckoned on finding out for himself the precise relationship they had with the courtesan. Under the guise of an avuncular interest he would scold them and in doing so study their reactions. Unfortunately for him this tactic, excellent though it might have been in some circumstances, was rendered ineffective for the reason that the young men in question, putting two and two together, had come to suspect an intimacy between him and Fernande and made up their minds to play on it. With the result that on the count's opening gambit of complaint that they should have been so thoughtless as to bring the courtesan into the respectable home of Madame de Barthèle, the gauntlet thrown down by him was instantly taken up, first by Léon de Vaux.

'Allow me, monsieur le comte,' he returned with no little irony, 'to protest at the prejudice you show against Madame Ducoudray.'

'Madame Ducoudray, Madame Ducoudray!' grumbled the peer. 'You know very well she is no more Madame Ducoudray than I am.'

'Of course I know it,' Léon returned, 'since it was we who invented it for the specific purpose of this occasion. All of which doesn't prevent her from being a charming woman. But as Fernande, surely you know something of her?' he insinuated.

'How should I know her?' the count demanded with some asperity.

'Why, as Fabien and I know her; as everyone knows her.'

'Not at all,' the count replied. 'I gave up such associations long ago.'

'All the same, there is a mystery surrounding her,' Fabien took over with a sly look at Léon. 'While poor Maurice here is wasting away from love of her, rumour has it that he has been succeeded by an invisible protector. What we want to know is, who can it be?'

'How should I know?' Monsieur de Montgiroux demanded, feeling on thorns.

'All that seems to be known about him', Léon put in, 'is that he arrives between one and two o'clock, when Fernande's door is pitilessly closed to everyone else. His carriage has been seen at the end of the courtyard, a carriage drawn by two chestnuts. Now among all your friends, Fabien, and your acquaintances, Monsieur le comte, who is there who has a carriage and two chestnut horses?'

'Why, Monsieur de Montgiroux of course,' said Madame de Barthèle who entered the room just in time to overhear Léon's awkward question.

'All the world has chestnut horses,' the count protested. 'It is the commonest colour. But now, dear madame,' he went on hurriedly, glad to change the train of conversation, 'how is our patient?'

'Wonderful!' Madame de Barthèle replied, radiating relief and joy. 'Madame Ducoudray has worked a miracle. She is a perfectly splendid woman!'

Smiles passed between the two young men, while a slight frown appeared on the count's forehead. 'Yes, splendid is the word,' the baroness repeated, remarking the two-fold effect of her words.

'And what exactly has she done to work this miracle?' the peer demanded a little testily.

'What has she done?' Madame de Barthèle exclaimed. 'She has put Maurice in the way of a complete cure. And if she will only stay the week the doctor, who is delighted with her, feels certain of a full return to health.'

'Stay the week, stay the week?' the count cried. 'Are you serious?'

'Certainly I am. I have just shown her to her rooms.'

'What! She is to stay here, in your house?'

'And where do you expect her to stay? At the hotel?'

'Under the same roof as Maurice?'

'Of course, since he is her patient.'

'But my niece! What about Clotilde?'

'She agrees entirely with me.'

'But think what people will say if all this becomes known.'

'People can think and say what they please, monsieur. My son is not in love with *people*. It is not *people* who can sing 'Ombra adorata' to him or bring him back to health.'

The argument between the count and the baroness was likely to have gone on still more warmly had not a carriage been heard to enter the courtyard. Then, before anyone could be sent to see who the newcomer might be and to say that no one could be received, a valet opened the door and announced Madame de Neuilly. At this name, which seemed to come as a justification of the count's worst fears, Madame de Barthèle turned pale. There was, however, nothing to be done. Madame de Neuilly was a relative, and it was not possible, and in any case too late, to debar her from being welcomed.

Madame de Neuilly was in her late twenties but looked considerably older, being tall and skinny, and with a face which, not made prepossessing in the first place by nature, in the second was even less so in being disfigured by smallpox. In short she was one of those persons for whom one is made to feel an instinctive revulsion. Devoid of the normal attractions of her sex she had come to making envy the mainspring of her thoughts, words and actions. She loved luxury and ostentatious display, but although coming from an old and highly ranked family, a mediocre fortune did not allow her to indulge her craving for such things, with the result that, as if in compensation for the deprivation, she had become a puritanically minded, backbiting, scandal-mongering woman. Never having been exposed to any attempt at seduction, she was pitiless to anyone who might have been weak enough to stray from the path of virtue.

Her cousin, Madame de Barthèle, was well aware of her

character and even more aware that her arrival at this juncture could not be seen other than as an unmitigated calamity. Nevertheless, there was nothing anyone could do but put on a good face and endeavour to hide the general embarrassment. But, experienced as the dowager was in the social graces, and although she at once came forward to greet her visitor in her most gracious manner, Madame de Neuilly saw at first glance that beneath her smile of welcome there lurked an expression of vexation.

'Ah, dear cousin!' she said after embracing her, 'I see I have dropped in at an awkward moment. I came in the hope of having lunch with you, but if I am *de trop* you must tell me, and I will go.

'No, no, my dear Cornélie!' the baroness protested in an effort to make the best of it. 'You know very well you are never *de trop* here. Of course you must stay.'

On entering the *salon* Madame de Neuilly at once took notice of the persons in it. 'No, no!' she insisted hypocritically, secretly determined more than ever by what she saw to remain. 'I see you already have Messieurs de Rieulle and de Vaux and the count. I thought I might catch you alone, especially after hearing what they are saying in Paris about you.'

'Oh, *mon Dieu!*' Madame de Barthèle exclaimed in alarm, 'what are they saying? Tell me.'

The trepidation displayed by the baroness only served to convince Madame de Neuilly that something out of the ordinary was happening here at Fontenay so, agog to fathom the mystery, she pursued as she fell into an armchair as though tired, 'They say, my dear cousin, that Maurice is very ill. Hence my surprise visit to see how he really is and to put myself at your service. But pray tell me, how is he? What is the matter with him?'

The air of concern put on by Madame de Neuilly contrasted so markedly with the expression on her face that the young men could not hide an involuntary smile, while the count made a gesture of impatience. In addition, the fact known to everyone that Madame de Neuilly had once evinced a passion for Maurice and hoped to become his wife, made the pantomime they were witnessing all the more comic in the eyes of all present. And it had been as a result of the failure of these hopes that she had later espoused a Monsieur de Neuilly, a sexagenarian, thought by her and everyone to be well-off but who, after only a few years of connubiality, had died. And as if to add to her ill luck the poor woman discovered that instead of a reasonable fortune as she had blissfully anticipated, he had put all his revenue into a life annuity.

In answer to Madame de Barthèle's explanation that Maurice was suffering from brain fever Madame de Neuilly declared, 'Brain fever? Well, really, your doctor must be stupid if he hasn't been able to cure him. You know, dear cousin, that I am well up in medical knowledge. I nursed Monsieur de Neuilly through his many illnesses until he died. So then, take me to see poor Maurice and I will tell you right away what his condition is and how to make him better.'

'It is very good of you, Cornélie,' the baroness put in hastily, 'and I am very touched by your concern and kind offer, but Maurice is asleep just now, and the doctor has sent us all away with orders that he is not on any account to be disturbed.'

'If he is sleeping, that is a good sign,' Madame de Neuilly conceded, with an authoritative air. 'But when he wakes you must let me see him for myself.'

As here was no way of escaping this inquisitorial visit it had to be endured. Madame de Barthèle and the count exchanged looks which told each other clearly of the suspicions likely to be aroused by a meeting between her cousin and the false Madame Ducoudray. And in fact the situation for the baroness was embarrassing in the extreme and put her on the horns of an awkward dilemma. Should she take her cousin into her confidence, or would it be better to leave her in ignorance of what Madame Ducoudray really was in the hope of getting away with it? If told the facts, she would be certain to make loud protest and shout infamy to high heaven. If left in ignorance and she then discovered the facts, that would prove to be worse since she would take offence and in return blazon the scandal to all Paris.

While she was weighing the pros and cons of the problem Clotilde entered.

'Lunch is ready,' she said to Madame de Barthèle, 'and I have just been and told Madame Ducoudray.'

Too late she remarked the presence of Madame de Neuilly, and understood the *faux pas* she had made. A silence followed her announcement, a silence felt by Madame de Neuilly to be one of embarrassment and which only served to increase her curiosity and add to her suspicions. Without so much as addressing Clotilde with the customary hypocritical greetings which women reserve for one another: '*Mon Dieu*!' she exclaimed, 'Who is this person, cousin? On arriving I observed a most elegant barouche with two fine horses. Would they be hers, by any chance?' Then realising that her remarks made before so much as speaking to Clotilde would be considered out of place, turning to her she said, 'Good day, dear Clotilde. I came to see how your husband is. Is this lady with him, may I ask?'

Her remarks came with such volubility that no one was able to put in a word. So it was that Clotilde, the last to be questioned, took it on herself to answer with: 'No, madame. Madame Ducoudray is certainly not with Maurice. She is in her room.'

'In her room!' cried Madame de Neuilly. 'So she is a guest, then, this Madame Ducoudray?'

'Madam,' Fabien hastened to explain, understanding the tortures the baroness and Clotilde were undergoing, 'Madame Ducoudray has been brought here by Léon and myself in the hope of bringing Maurice back to health.'

'Bringing Maurice back to health?' Madame de Neuilly echoed. 'Is this Madame Ducoudray some homeopath, then?'

'No, madame,' said Fabien. 'Quite simply, if you must know, she is a hypnotist.'

'Really!' cried Madame de Neuilly, enchanted. 'How splendid! I have always wanted to meet a hypnotist. But she must be very much *à la mode* to have a carriage and pair of her own.'

Taken aback by the succession of untruths forced on them by the prying questions of Madame de Neuilly, the persons involved looked round at one another uneasily until Fabien, taking the initiative, said to Madame de Barthèle, 'Madame, would you be good enough to take me to the hypnotist. She is, I know, extraordinarily susceptible to outside influences, and the sudden appearance of someone else – with all respect to Madame de Neuilly' – this said with a polite bow to that lady – 'might be upsetting to her.'

Madame de Barthèle understood instantly the young man's purpose, and breathing again, 'Yes, yes, of course,' she hastened to approve. 'Clotilde, take Monsieur de Rieulle's arm and show him to Madame Ducoudray's room. And perhaps you will persuade her to come and have lunch with us.'

Clotilde took Fabien's arm with some hesitation, trembling slightly. But as they moved towards the door it was opened, and Fernande stood on the threshold. On seeing her Madame de Neuilly uttered a cry of astonishment, a cry which resounded in the ears and on the hearts of all there with a sense of warning that some new and unexpected development was about to unfold.

* * *

The alarm caused by Madame de Neuilly's cry was changed to astonishment when that pillar of respectability and morality was seen to go up to the courtesan with a smile of recognition exclaiming, 'What! Is it really you, dear Fernande?' As to Fernande, acting as though no fresh emotion could shake her, she let Madame de Neuilly embrace her without showing anything but a pleased surprise.

'*Mon Dieu!*' Madame de Neuilly continued ecstatically,

'how happy I am to meet you after all these years! And to find you more lovely than ever! Tell me, what have you been doing with yourself since we last saw each other? As for me, I have married, but now, alas, I am a widow. I married a Monsieur de Neuilly who was considerably older than I: not as a speculation, let me tell you, as he had placed his revenue in life annuities, leaving me little enough. But there you are, you see. That is how life goes.'

All the time she was pouring out her story she eyed with envy the beauty, the distinguished air, dress and elegance of her former friend; then turning to Madame de Barthèle: 'You must forgive this personal greeting, dear cousin,' she said, 'but I cannot begin to tell you what a joy it is for me to meet again my most cherished companion of Saint-Denis.'

'Of Saint-Denis!' was repeated in astonishment by those looking on at this scene.

'Yes, Saint-Denis! You did not know of that, apparently. You see, Fernande and I were educated there, and in the same classes. And close friends let me tell you! I knew all about her. Her father was a brave officer killed on the battlefield. I see you know nothing of all this. Let me introduce you, then, to the girl I knew as Mademoiselle de –'

'No, no!' Fernande interrupted her flow. 'Please – no! I don't want my father's name to be mentioned.'

'But why ever not, my dear? Are you some queen travelling incognito, by any chance? Your name is one to be proud of, and I cannot understand why the daughter of the Marquis de Mormant ...'

But here Fernande uttered a cry of grief, while her face reflected the shame and anger she felt at this exposure of her family name so carefully guarded by her. When she could bring herself to speak it was to expostulate, 'You have done me a bad turn, madame. I did not want it to be known who my father was.'

'But in that case, my dear Fernande, tell me why you should want that.'

'The simple fact is,' Fernande replied in a melancholy

–76–

voice, 'we are no longer in that place where we passed our happiest years. Much water has flowed under the bridge since then – alas!'

'Of course you were happy there. I remember it used to be said that you were the most talented and beautiful of all of us.'

'Fatal attributes, those!' Fernande exclaimed with a significant look at the three men who were looking on in silence.

'But it was because of your accomplishments that everyone predicted a splendid marriage and future for you,' the widow persisted. 'And surely it seems as though our predictions have been proved right. What! an expensive elegant carriage of your own, two splendid horses – what more? He is well off, then, your Monsieur Duponderay … Dufonderay … I forget. What is your husband's name?'

'Ducoudray,' Fernande affirmed, resigning herself to the need to keep up the deceit.

'Ducoudray!' Madame de Neuilly repeated. 'Ah well! I hope he is better able to leave you comfortably off than my husband was, with his income placed in life annuities. It is no small matter, I can tell you, when one has been brought up with a taste for the little luxuries of life: no more living in hotels, no more carriages, no more horses. But, forgive me for coming back to the subject, what I cannot understand is why you should be so unwilling to let it be known who your father was when, as I know, he bore so honourable a name. But no doubt you have your reasons.'

'Naturally I have my reasons,' Fernande replied shortly, 'and you have hurt me greatly by divulging it after I had particularly asked you not to so do. Still, for the sake of our old friendship, I forgive you.'

'Really!' Madame de Neuilly exclaimed, hurt by Fernande's rejoinder, 'I did not expect this cold welcome from an old schoolfriend.'

'You are mistaken,' Fernande answered her accusation in a humble tone. 'But Madame de Barthèle understands why I have no option but to act as I am doing, which does not prevent her from accepting me as I am.'

'Certainly not, my dear,' the baroness intervened, seeing her cue and quite charmed by the calm and dignified way Fernande was parrying Madame de Neuilly's inquisition. 'And I can say to my cousin that I find you to be one of the most delightful people I have ever had the pleasure of meeting.'

'In that case,' her cousin took her up, 'why couldn't she tell me about herself as I have done?'

Fortunately for Fernande and everyone the lunch bell sounded, making it unnecessary for Madame de Neuilly's question to be answered, and the baroness seized on the fact to break up the scene by saying, 'You hear, everyone? Lunch is ready. Let us leave confidences until later. We have all the afternoon for that. Monsieur de Vaux, please give your arm to Madame Ducoudray. Monsieur le Comte, yours to Madame de Neuilly.' Fabien in the meantime had already proffered his to Clotilde. In this way everyone made their way into the dining-room. Once at table, Madame de Barthèle placed the count on her left and Fernande on her right; Léon next to Fernande, Madame de Neuilly opposite her with Fabien on her right; and lastly Clotilde between Fabien and the count.

The secret of Fernande's birth and background so unexpectedly revealed by Madame de Neuilly's indiscretion was naturally in the forefront of everyone's thoughts and especially in those of the baroness, led by it to congratulate herself on her perspicacity in having from the first perceived in the courtesan a woman of good birth and breeding. Furthermore it helped to explain and mitigate in her mind her son's guilty passion for her.

As may well be imagined the revelation had no less an effect on Monsieur de Montgiroux, now beginning to discover hitherto unsuspected qualities in his mistress, and this in turn inducing certain hitherto dubious ideas concerning her and their relationship. Seduced by the newly-discovered secret of her social rank, and convincing himself that neither Léon nor Fabien nor, for that matter, Maurice, had possessed her, the idea gradually took hold of him to make her something more than a mistress: in fact to give her his name and so make sure of her in a more moral and permanent fashion.

For his part Léon, far from feeling his hopes of making her his mistress diminished, determined to press his claim even more strongly. Fabien alone was unmoved by the revelation, being still full of his intention to conquer the docile Clotilde who, it must be said, now that her fears for her husband's health were proving unfounded, relaxed, and listened to the young man's voice with a reluctant pleasure as something new.

Madame de Neuilly, urged by her jealous envy of anyone who might be thought superior to her in beauty or fortune, sought persistently in her mind as to the reason Fernande might have for not wishing her real name to be divulged, and suspecting some clandestine intrigue, some deliberately hidden secret, made up her mind she would not leave the house until she had unravelled it.

For Fernande, only resilience of spirit enabled her to persevere with the imbroglio in which she found herself, and by force of will to rise above the emotional atmosphere around her. Thus steeled, she was able to see through the schemes of Fabien, the tentative reciprocation of Clotilde, the aroused hopes of Léon, the thwarted spite of Madame de Neuilly, and the agitation of the count.

In the midst of these different emotions it was difficult for the group to keep up a general conversation even though each one was anxious to keep his secret thoughts hidden from the rest. It was of course Madame de Neuilly who set the ball rolling.

'I hope, dear Fernande,' she began, 'you are not so taken up by your séances that you no longer find time to devote yourself to your painting. I remember how the drawing master at Saint-Denis used to declare he would not be sorry if you were to lose your fortune so that you could be made to become an artist.'

'Really!' the baroness exclaimed. 'Madame paints?'

'Yes, indeed,' Léon observed, anxious to ingratiate himself with Fernande. 'I myself can vouch for it. She is a first-rate artist and could exhibit if she so desired.'

The count regarded his mistress with growing astonishment, seeing in her not merely a courtesan but a woman of unsuspected talent. So it was that, partly from genuine interest, partly from a desire on the part of everyone to avoid personal matters, a discussion on aesthetics ensued arising from their learning of Fernande's artistic talent and in the course of which she was asked to give her opinion on various painters, composers and writers. In response to her naming Shakespeare as being among the greatest of the last category, Madame de Neuilly interjected, 'My dear Fernande, how can you possibly admire that foreign barbarian?'

'That barbarian, as you call him,' Fernande riposted, 'is the man who has created most after God.'

'Do you know, dear Madame Ducoudray,' the baroness confessed, 'it has never occurred to me to read Shakespeare!'

'Sheer ingratitude, madame! We women above all should make a cult of him.'

'And why so?' Madame de Barthèle demanded, intrigued.

'Because he has created the most admirable examples of our sex. Juliet, Miranda, Desdemona, Rosalind, Perdita are types of women we must all admire.'

'Count,' the baroness said turning to Monsieur de Montgiroux, 'you are going to Paris this evening, I believe. Please bring me back a Shakespeare.'

'I would with the greatest pleasure,' he replied, 'but I have decided against going after all. I feel my presence is necessary here.'

'But you told me you had promised your colleagues you would be there,' she insisted. 'And now that Maurice is well on the way to recovery –'

'Nevertheless, madame, I am going back on my promise, and when they know the reasons I am sure they will forgive me.'

'Oh, monsieur le comte,' observed Léon who appeared to have taken it on himself to harass the peer, 'surely you will not deprive your colleagues of your all-important presence? Duty before pleasure, and all that?'

The count only smiled while saying to himself, 'He wants to get me out of the way. We will see!'

At this point the baroness rose and led the way into the garden where they were to have their coffee. Taking advantage of the general movement the count approached Fernande and said in a low voice 'You understand, don't you. It is for your sake I am staying. I must have words with you.'

She was about to reply when a cry from Madame de Barthèle made her turn and look round, to see Maurice who, profiting from the absence of the doctor who had left to make a visit to another of his patients, made his way downstairs and now, pale and weak and clad in a dressing gown, stood in the doorway.

Five

Five

The crisis foreseen by Doctor Gaston had happily been passed. Maurice had slept for nearly three hours, and during this beneficent sleep, long since stranger to him, the turbulence in his blood had eased. On waking he had tried to unravel his as yet obscure thoughts and recollections in which Fernande remained the central but elusive clue, a guiding thread leading him through the labyrinth of his confused ideas. He seemed to recall that she had suddenly appeared before him, sung to him, spoken to him. But how, he asked himself, was it possible for his mistress to be here, in the same house as his wife and mother? Surely that must have been one of his feverish dreams ….

Driven by an overwhelming desire to clear up the mystery, and feeling refreshed after his sleep, he got out of bed. At first, as he stood, he swayed unsteadily; then shortly a modicum of strength returned and he was able to take a few steps around the room. A glance in the mirror of his dressing-table showed him an emaciated figure with a drawn face, unkempt beard, tousled hair and preternaturally bright, dark-shadowed eyes. After combing his hair and beard he tottered over to the wardrobe, found a dressing-gown and put it on; then slowly and shakily he made his way to the door and so along the corridor and down the stairs, holding on to the banister rail as he went. As he approached the dining-room he heard the sound of voices, and as he stopped and listened intently he was sure he heard Fernande's voice; that vibrant remembered voice. Convinced that her presence was not just a figment of his imagination, he turned the handle and pushed open the door.

At the cry uttered by his mother he suddenly became aware of the proprieties. A first glance had shown him Fernande, then grouped around her his mother, his wife, Monsieur de Montgiroux, Madame de Neuilly, Fabien and Léon. At the sight of them he became intimidated, and like a child caught in the wrong he had recourse to seeking to deceive himself in order to deceive others.

'*Mon Dieu*, Maurice!' his mother exclaimed as she hurried over to him and took his arm. 'What imprudence!'

'Don't worry, mother,' he replied. 'I feel a lot better; only I'm dying for a breath of fresh air.'

'Well, well!' came the voice of Doctor Gaston behind him, returned from his visit. 'So our patient is on his feet again! Since he feels the need of air, let him have it. The weather is in favour. Coffee in the garden, then, ladies, if you please. A patient who can walk is halfway on the road to recovery.'

He took Maurice's arm and led the way into the garden. Clotilde hurried on ahead to make preparations to have the siesta in an arbour shaded by acacia and maple trees where everyone could sit at ease. The others followed, each with his or her own thoughts. The count was desperate to be alone with Fernande. Madame de Neuilly, not having as yet had the opportunity of conversing with her, promised herself a series of questions so thorny that be she as subtle as she may, some tissues of truth would be brought to light.

It was now Maurice's turn to be led from one surprise to another. In addition to having Fernande received openly by his wife and mother, he was amazed even more by seeing her arm in arm and chatting familiarly with Madame de Neuilly – that straight-laced prude so friendly with his mistress, the courtesan Fernande! Then without intent his mother proceeded to throw him into further bewilderment. Fearing that Madame de Neuilly's persistent questioning would weary Fernande and perhaps lead her to drop words which would betray the truth about herself, she deliberately broke into their conversation.

'Come now, ladies,' she intervened with the authority of her age and as hostess, 'Have a thought for our poor invalid. You are walking too fast.' And turning to the three men who were bringing up the rear, 'Really, gentlemen!' she scolded them, 'What has come over you? Monsieur de Rieulle, have you by any chance quarrelled with Madame de Neuilly? And you, Monsieur de Vaux, have you nothing to say to Madame Ducoudray?'

The count made as if to follow Fabien and Léon, but the baroness seized his arm. 'One moment, Count. You are of our party. Stay behind with us, if you please.'

'My dear cousin,' said Madame de Neuilly who was longing to have Fernande to herself, 'pray do not bother about us. We have such a lot to talk about, Madame Ducoudray and I.'

This was the second time the name of Madame Ducoudray had been pronounced in Maurice's hearing, leaving him more than ever mystified.

'And what will you talk about?' Madame de Barthèle pressed her cousin.

'About hypnotism, to be sure. I want to know more about the science.'

Fernande, hypnotist? This was one more enigma for Maurice to add to the others.

'That may be so,' the dowager took her cousin up, 'but I see no reason why that need deprive the rest of us of Madame Ducoudray's company.'

'Oh yes, yes indeed, cousin!' Madame de Neuilly insisted. 'Besides, we have reminiscences of schooldays to chat about. Two old friends like us, who haven't seen each other for years, naturally have a whole lot of confidences to exchange.'

Madame de Neuilly and Fernande schoolfriends? Fernande then must have been at Saint-Denis, that ultra-fashionable *pension*, which in turn meant that she must have come from a well-born family. Here was more matter for Maurice to ponder over.

By this time the little party had reached the arbour where Clotilde was waiting for them and where they were to take their coffee. A table had been prepared and chairs and an armchair for Maurice placed round it. They took their places more or less at random. In doing so Léon was separated from Fernande; Fabien found himself next to Madame de Neuilly; Maurice in the armchair was between his mother and the doctor; the count next to Madame de Barthèle, with Clotilde, who had been standing and directing the servants, having no option but to take the vacant chair between the count and Fernande. Superficially it was a scene of contentment and tranquillity, a scene, too, seemingly blessed by nature for the benefit of the invalid. The afternoon sun, gradually declining but still warm in the first days of May, filtered its rays through the branches; scarcely a breeze stirred the leaves. Two swans were indolently swimming in a distant lake which reflected the blue of the sky like a mirror. For the first time in his life Maurice was experiencing that miraculous sensation of well-being, that sense of returning to normal health known only to those who have recovered from a serious illness.

Placed as she was beside Fernande, Clotilde felt obliged during the general conversation over coffee to pay some attention to her rival for Maurice's love. Yet to talk hypocritically about trivialities seemed to her impossible. Bracing herself, therefore, and speaking in a voice only Fernande could hear she said, 'I am sorry you are being harassed by Madame de Neuilly. We never expected her. But believe me, we are grateful, in spite of everything, for what you are doing here.'

'And believe me, madame,' Fernande returned, 'I am happy to know that I am being of some use.'

'Both his mother and I will never forget it is you who, though you abandoned Maurice and so were the cause of his illness, came and brought him back to life.'

'I did not abandon Monsieur de Barthèle, madame. I simply learned that he was married, that is all. Yes, I loved him. But from the moment I knew he was married, well, that was the end.'

'What! Did you not know he was married?'

'On my honour, no! And now that I have met you, his wife, surely you must realise that after concluding my duty here it will mark the end more than ever.'

Touched by this self-sacrifice and devotion Clotilde seized Fernande's hand and pressed it warmly.

*   *   *

As the afternoon declined and one of those treacherous breezes of early May began to freshen, the doctor considered it wise to take Maurice indoors. This being rather against the patient's wish, after discussion it was generally agreed by way of compensation that after a short interval they would all meet once more in his room. In the meantime his mother and Clotilde went with him and the doctor to see him back in bed; Fabien and Léon began smoking cigars as they strolled around the garden; and finally the count, seizing his anxiously sought opportunity, approaching Fernande, whispered in her ear, 'Can you come back here in half an hour's time?'

'Yes,' she promised.

'Now then, what was all that?' Madame de Neuilly demanded, approaching Fernande in her turn.

'Nothing, madame,' the count replied. 'I was asking madame if she was thinking of returning to Paris this evening.' And with a bow to the two ladies he walked away with the intention of joining Fabien and Léon. But on the way back he was accosted by Madame de Barthèle.

'Where are you going, count?' she demanded. On his stating his purpose she went on, 'Not at all, not at all! The doctor has ordered us all inside now that it is turning cooler, and as a friend careful of your health I am asking you to give me your arm and to find the ladies. Where are they? In the billiards room? Or the conservatory, perhaps?'

'In the conservatory, I believe.'

'Well then, let us go and join them.'

There was no way the count could refuse the invitation, and trying to conceal a thwarted expression he gave her his arm and they went off in search of Fernande and Madame de Neuilly.

Meanwhile Clotilde, who had left her husband in the hands of his *valet de chambre*, took her way downstairs with a vague distress at heart. Once alone with her Maurice had taken her hands and kissed them gratefully, but no more. Before these dramatic events she would have gone on believing she was secure of his love, but her contact with Fernande had undeceived her, had awakened her in fact to the difference there was between simple conjugal affection and passionate desire. So it was that the young inexperienced wife, full of these burning thoughts, wished for nothing but to find solitude in order to sort out her emotions, and with this in mind she made her way to the little arbour where she had served the coffee and sat next to Fernande. There she turned her thoughts unwillingly, but nevertheless turned them, to Fabien, a man who had confessed to being in love with her. Could this be the same kind of love Maurice had for Fernande? she asked herself. A shudder ran through her at the thought.

She was at this stage of her reflections when a footstep behind her made her start. By the sudden beating of her heart she knew without turning that it was Fabien de Rieulle. Her first impulse was to run away, but her feet seemed to have taken root.

'Madame,' he began, coming close to her, 'this is surely a moment of Providence! I felt an irresistible urge to come back to the spot where I last saw you, and find you here before me. Could it be a case of mutual empathy?'

'Monsieur,' Clotilde replied, shaken by new emotions, 'I have just left my husband and come here to be alone. Permit me, then, to leave you.'

'But surely there can be solitude for two as well as one,' Fabien observed. 'And for that all that is needed are two hearts with a single thought between them.'

'For that', Clotilde rejoined, 'you would have to know what my thoughts were.'

'But I can read them, I am sure.'

'Well then, perhaps you will tell me what you read.'

'I will try, madame. To begin with I see sadness, and a wound. Why? Because you are suffering from a sense of outrage. You imagined – forgive me if I speak frankly – you had Maurice's undivided love; but with his illness and the arrival of its cause, that is to say his mistress, and your realisation of his passion for her, your mind has been thrown into a state of turmoil. Have I not read you aright?'

The young, inexperienced and artless Clotilde looked at him in amazement, struck wordless by the accuracy of his analysis. He understood her and repressed a smile of triumph.

'You are no doubt wondering how I have been able to read your heart in this way,' Fabien pursued. 'The answer is easy. It is simply because I feel a real love for you, a love such as you deserve to have but have not obtained, that is all.'

'Ah, Monsieur de Rieulle!' she murmured, 'you should not be speaking to me like this. You are Maurice's friend, and I am his wife.'

'And haven't I respected that friendship?' Fabien demanded quickly. 'All the time Maurice was dancing attendance on his mistress, did I betray him? Do me that much justice, madame. And for my love, do you think I have loved you only from today? No, I have loved you ever since I first met you as Maurice's friend. But again, did I let you know?'

'No, no!' she protested, forcing herself to resist the power of his looks and words. 'If I were to let myself listen to you we should both be guilty. Please, please leave me. Let me go – go back to my husband.'

'Go back to your husband?' he cried disdainfully. 'Do you imagine he really wants you at his bedside? Undeceive yourself, madame. Someone else will be there; someone else will be consoling him ...'

'You are mistaken, monsieur,' a woman's severe voice broke in. 'That someone else is here.'

Both Clotilde and Fabien uttered an exclamation of surprise. 'Fernande!' Clotilde cried.

'So, you were eavesdropping, madame!' Fabien accused her.

'Say rather I happened to overhear you as I was going past,' Fernande rejoined.

'Well and good! All the same, your place is hardly here, I fancy. It should be with Maurice, surely?' His tone was sarcastic.

'My place is wherever it happens to be needed, monsieur, and at the moment it happens to be here.'

'You were brought here because of Maurice,' Fabien retorted, 'and not for anyone else.'

'This morning I was fortunate enough to save him. Now I am saving his honour.'

'Oh yes, you are right!' Clotilde exclaimed as Fernande's words began to make clear to her the gulf into which she was on the verge of throwing herself.

'You are taking too much on yourself, Madame Moralist!' Fabien said, seizing Fernande's wrist in a threatening gesture.

But she, without showing any sense of intimidation, went on, 'You seem to forget that a young girl who is seduced is only temporarily dishonoured; a married woman who betrays her husband is a woman lost once and for all. You see, madame, Monsieur de Rieulle has no reply to that.'

'That is only because I am struck dumb by your audacity,' he said.

'You are right, a hundred times right!' Clotilde confessed. 'Take me away from here, please.'

Fernande answered her appeal by taking her hand and leading her away, leaving Fabien motionless with resentment and thwarted design. The two women walked on until, after re-entering the house, they found a sort of boudoir in an isolated wing of the château lighted feebly by a single alabaster lamp. Fernande pointed to a chair, but before seating herself she carefully closed the door.

'Now we can talk without fear of being interrupted,' she said.

'Oh, Fernande!' Clotilde exclaimed gratefully, 'You have saved me in a weak moment. First Maurice, then me! How can I thank you?'

'By not letting yourself become what I have become.'

'How is it you have so much influence over us? What sort of woman are you really?'

'Do you really wish to know?' Fernande said in a tone of infinite sadness.

'Oh yes! I feel certain I can learn something from what you tell me.'

'Well, that is to the good. And it will give me some relief to talk to someone who I know will listen with sympathy. And God knows for five years I have gone without that.'

'Of course I will listen, if only in exchange for all you have done for us here,' Clotilde said fervently, and pressed the other's hand in a spontaneous gesture of sympathy.

'Very well, then. Listen, and I will try to tell you everything,' Fernande responded.

There followed a silence during which Fernande, her head bowed, sat motionless. At last, as if bracing herself to narrate the painful recollections she had promised her listener, she raised her head.

'Pray don't imagine', she began, 'that I have the intention of seeking to excuse my behaviour by claiming qualities I do not possess or recounting dangers I have never run. No. No one, I assure you, could be more severe on myself than I am. All the same, I do believe that a woman rarely falls from virtue without having been pushed by another, or others, into that fault. We are formed by nature to attract the other sex, and at the same time we receive an education – so-called –

which leaves us in complete ignorance of evil and hopelessly open to the wiles of men. At least that has been my experience.

'I lost my mother while I was still in my cradle, and was brought up by persons who had little more than a mercenary interest in me. I knew nothing of those maternal cares which prepare a girl for the problems she has to face. The only knowledge of my parentage I had was passed on to me in vague, disinterested terms by the various women who were paid to look after me; and the only facts I learned were that I was born in the old Breton château of Mormant, and that my father was a marquis and a colonel in the Bourbon army fighting against Napoleon, and that my mother died bringing me into the world.'

'It is a sad fact, but we have much in common,' Clotilde observed. 'Like you I lost my mother more or less at the same time and in similar circumstances.'

'Yes, no doubt, madame. But there the similarity of our destinies ends, fortunately for you.' Then with a deep sigh Fernande continued: 'Through the ups and downs of fortune which I never understood, my father was forced to sell the Breton château of his ancestors and to live in modest apartments in Paris. I was taken to join him there, but I saw little enough of him, called away as he was by military service. My most vivid memory of that time is when one day the woman who had charge of me told me that my father was dead, killed while fighting with the army in Spain. But I was too young for the full impact of the news to make itself felt on me, and besides, I scarely knew my father. Eventually it was discovered he had made a will by which I was left the little he had, and for guardian and so to speak step-father in his place, a certain Comte de —, a brother-in-arms.

'To do him justice, at first the count carried out my father's wishes. I was sent, when I was old enough, to that most élite of boarding schools, Saint-Denis, for which he paid the fees. However, during those six years I scarcely ever saw this guardian. He did come to see me there once or twice to find out how I was getting on, and I dutifully wrote him an occasional letter, but that was all.

'Then when I was sixteen, all that changed. As you can imagine, at that age I was no longer a dowdy pupil in dowdy clothes but a young woman, tall for my age and well developed. One day the count happened to call at the *pension* to have a word with me. On seeing me and talking to me I sensed a difference in his attitude. He no longer patted me on the head and spoke down to me. I saw his eyes light up as he examined me, and he spoke to me and treated me as a grown woman. In fact he began playing the gallant and paying me compliments, telling me how beautiful and attractive and altered I had become. At that time he would be, as far as I can recall, between forty-five and fifty. Of course I knew nothing of his character or way of life, and knew nothing about men; and it was not until later – too late, alas! – that I learned he was a roué and a habitué of several of the many dissolute clubs of the capital. All I know is that from that time on he came to see me more and more often, spoke of the gay life of Paris, and when the time came for me to leave the *pension* persuaded me to live with him as his ward in his apartments. But I did so with regret. I had become attached to the place and the teachers there (and incidentally it was there I met and got to know Madame de Neuilly, or Mademoiselle Cornélie de Morcerf as she was known then) and above all to my painting and music in which, so I was told, I had more than average talent. But then I was completely in his power, being utterly dependent on him financially.

'To begin with all was well. To keep the proprieties the count engaged a sort of housekeeper to see to all my wants and to chaperone me. But it soon became apparent even to one of my innocence that she was in his pay. Whenever he came to visit me – and his visits became more and more frequent – it was to ask if he could take me out with him to the theatre, to a ball, to any sort of amusement; in fact, if she saw me to be hesitant or unwilling, she would urge me to oblige him, pointing out that my livelihood, my very existence, depended on his kindness.

'So, gradually, he became more and more familiar, and I began to succumb to the pleasures of society I indulged in with him. Finally, to cut a long story short, one day he threw himself at my feet and confessed he loved me. For some time I held out. I didn't really love him. For one thing our ages were too disparate; for another, I was too young, too naive for love. But undeterred he persisted until at last, wearied by his reproaches and demands, and urged on cynically by my so-called chaperone, I gave way to him. In short, seduced by him, I became his mistress.'

Clotilde could not suppress a cry at the brusque avowal; but then, anxious to repair the instinctive reprobation she felt she had unintentionally expressed, she essayed some words of self-excuse.

'Oh, don't excuse yourself,' Fernande interjected. 'No doubt you consider me to be worthy of pity. I might have been so had I gone no further. But almost before I became aware of what was happening to me I found myself living in a world of pleasure and cynical enjoyment. The count, revelling in showing me off to his friends and associates, took me to all his gay abandoned amusements, and I lived a life of luxury and brilliance, indifferent to the future and slowly becoming dead to shame and almost as depraved as he was. This went on for three years.

'But then came the terrible cholera epidemic. The count was one of its first victims. On his death I discovered that he had left me most of what remained of his fortune after being squandered in dissipation – enough to live on had I practised the strictest economy and lived a life of abstinence and restraint. But see how the past influences our present! I had become so degenerate, so accustomed to a life of gaiety and luxury, that I knew I was unable to face such an existence. Whereupon I went from bad to worse, living the life of a courtesan – until I met Maurice.'

Despite her self-control Clotilde felt a shudder of apprehension at the stark avowal from Fernande of her love for her husband. The courtesan saw and understood it.

'Oh, you have nothing to fear now,' she continued. 'True, it is to Maurice I owe my regeneration and the happiest later months of my life. But now that is all over.'

A silence ensued, a silence during which Clotilde, much moved, took the hand Fernande had half stretched out to her and held it in her own. At last, withdrawing her hand and looking at her companion with an appealing air Fernande went on, 'You have, I hope, learned something from my story. Let me conclude with a further warning. You will remember, I am sure, the dreadful scandal round the name of the young, fashionable and beautiful Baronne de Villefort.'

'Something, but not all the details.'

'I will fill them in for you, briefly. For one reason or another the baroness fancied her husband no longer loved her. A young man, a friend of both her and her husband, decided to take advantage of this. After some weeks she foolishly gave way to his protestations and declarations of love and became his mistress, only to find out that he was no better than other men and was deceiving her with other women. In the end she begged him to free her and to return some letters she had written to him. He refused. In despair she confessed everything to her husband. He challenged the other to a duel, and was killed. That true story should be a warning to all married women.'

'But her lover,' Clotilde asked, 'who was he?'

'His name is Fabien de Rieulle.'

Clotilde uttered a cry of horror at the sudden and unexpected revelation. Fernande, thinking to leave her alone to ponder over her story, got up and made for the door. But on the threshold she found herself confronted by Madame de Neuilly.

Six

Six

'Ah! There you are!' exclaimed that lady. 'Found at last! I have been looking all over for you, *ma chère*. And where in heaven's name is Clotilde?'

'Here I am,' said Clotilde, coming forward. 'Do you want me for anything?'

'Good heavens! Can't one want to see somebody without having a reason for it? I merely want to have a chat with my old schoolfriend, though in truth she doesn't seem very anxious to reciprocate.'

'Madame,' Fernande hastened to reply, determined to keep a distance between the importunate Madame de Neuilly and herself, 'one of the steps I resolved to take on renouncing my family name was never to renew association with any I used to know in my happier days.'

'What do you mean, *ma chère*, talking about happier days? What more do you need in order to be happy? You have your carriage and horses, servants, a suite in one of the finest quarters in Paris — everything, it seems to me.'

Fernande shuddered on learning that the other had somehow found out her address.

'My dear cousin,' Clotilde observed, seeing how much this inquisition was troubling Fernande, 'you will remember that we are to assemble in Maurice's room for some music. Madame de Barthèle and Monsieur de Montgiroux are perhaps already there waiting for us.'

'There you are quite wrong, my dear,' the widow replied.

'At this very moment they are arguing with one another in the *salon*.'

'Arguing?' Clotilde questioned, forcing a laugh in the hope of diverting the conversation from Fernande. 'What are they arguing about?'

'How should I know? I gather Monsieur de Montgiroux was wanting to go out, perhaps to look for you as I was doing, but madame was insisting that he stayed inside with her.'

Her words recalled to Fernande the count's impatient desire to see her, and having no reason for refusing him his wish she made a move towards the door. But it was never easy for anyone to escape the clutches of Madame de Neuilly.

'Well, *chère petite*, what are you doing?' she protested. 'Everyone seems to have developed a passion for walking about today. Here are you wanting to perambulate, Monsieur de Montgiroux wants to take a stroll, Monsieur Léon and Monsieur Fabien are wandering about in the garden, and here am I infected with the general mania. If you like, while Clotilde goes to see if Maurice is ready to receive us, I will accompany you wherever you want to go.'

'Thank you,' Fernande replied politely but firmly, 'but much as I appreciate your kind offer, I must leave you. I have some orders I must give to my people. I will join you later in the *salon*.'

And here, after a cool reverence, she went off with an air which told Madame de Neuilly clearly that she would disoblige her strongly if she insisted on going with her. The widow watched her go. Then, when she was out of sight, 'Her people!' she muttered. 'Madame Ducoudray has *people* to give orders to, while I ... And when I think that if Monsieur de Neuilly hadn't put all his income into life annuities I too would have had people to give instructions to! I would very much like to know what she has to say to her *people*.'

'Probably to tell them to have her carriage ready,' Clotilde suggested, overhearing the other's muttered insinuations.

−102−

'Her carriage ready? But I thought you said she was to spend the night here.'

'So she intended; but probably the annoyances she has been subjected to since she arrived this morning have made her change her mind.'

'Annoyances? Who is there here to cause her annoyances, may I ask? I hope you are not referring to me when you say that, my dear Clotilde.'

'Not at all, dear cousin; though to speak truth I do think your cross-questionings have put her out.'

'Embarrassed her, no doubt you mean. But it is all so simple. I meet in her an old schoolfriend, so of course I want to know what has happened to her since those days. I find she is married to a Monsieur Ducoudray. Naturally I am curious to know something about him and her. Purely friendly interest. When I ceased to bear my maiden name of Morcerf to take that of de Neuilly I was prepared to tell the whole world about him if asked. You know that, don't you, cousin?'

* * *

In the meantime Fernande, who as we have seen had made up her mind to cold-shoulder her officious former friend, after leaving her took her way into the garden and towards the little arbour where coffee had been taken earlier in the afternoon. By this time the sun was low in the sky, and rosy streaks laced the higher branches of the trees. On walking along the path which led to the desired spot, hearing the voices of Léon and Fabien who happened to be strolling there smoking their cigars, and not wishing to meet them, she took another path which seemed to lead in the same direction. She walked quickly, certain that the count would be waiting for her in a state of agitation and suspense; but gradually her steps became slower as a growing complexity of emotions began to play havoc in her mind. What would his attitude to her be now? she asked herself. Would he not reproach her for being the cause of Maurice's passion and illness? But, came her answer, how could she have known that? that he still loved her as she loved him? that it was, as he thought, his unreciprocated love that was eating at his heart and his very will to go on living? These questionings in turn brought back in spite of all her will the forlorn hope that, knowing now that they still loved each other, and more, that his love for his wife amounted to affection and respect but no more, they might renew their broken *liaison*. And finally, should she use the present situation to break altogether with the count?

Alas! Our story is not so much a narrative of events as a drama of analysis. It is a moral autopsy we have undertaken; and just as in the most healthy body there is some lesion through which death will sooner or later strike, so the most generous and noble of hearts hide imperfect fibres which demonstrate that mankind is composed of virtuous and lofty ideas and ignoble actions. Thus it was with Fernande. These refractory thoughts lying in the depths of her heart but kept at bay while in the presence of Maurice's wife and mother, now that she found herself alone and in the knowledge that he still loved her, these thoughts rose to the surface with relentless intensity.

It was, then, as a prey to this tormenting flux of emotions that she approached the arbour. But the sound of voices from it brought her to a sudden stop as, listening, she recognised those of the count and Madame de Barthèle. However watchful the baroness had been, Monsieur de Montgiroux had been able to make his escape while she was conversing with the doctor, and had made his way with all possible speed to his rendezvous with his mistress. But as intimated, Fernande, first delayed by making a detour to avoid Léon and Fabien, and then by the weight of her thoughts, was not there when he arrived. He therefore waited impatiently in the early dusk of the evening. And soon the rustle of a dress told him of a woman's approach.

'At last you are here!' he cried, hurrying to greet her. 'I

seem to have been waiting hours. Surely you understand how important it is for me to have words with you. Now, will you be good enough to give me an explanation of what is going on here?'

But to the count's astonishment and dismay a voice other than Fernande's replied, 'I think it is for you, Count, to do the explaining of this strange rendezvous.'

'*Mon Dieu*! It is you, madame,' he exclaimed.

'Yes, monsieur. It is I – I whom you little expected, I am sure. Now then, perhaps you will be good enough to tell me what there is between you and Madame Ducoudray, or rather, Fernande. Where have you met her? Where have you got to know her? Come! the truth if you please!'

'Madame,' the count stammered lamely, pushed at the first throw into his defences, 'are you seriously intending to play the jealous woman with me?'

'Very seriously, monsieur. For some time now I have given credence to your excuses of ministerial meetings and such-like stories. But credulity has its limits, and what I have seen with my own eyes today has enlightened me.'

'But what in heaven's name do you imagine you have seen?' the count demanded, shaken but temporising.

'I will tell you. I have seen that this Fernande is young, attractive and, so it is said, far from niggardly in exercising her charms. I have observed your agitation when she first arrived, and the signs of recognition between the two of you. And now I find you here obviously expecting her. I think I merit an explanation; for you know very well, Count, that despite your infidelities I have never been unfaithful to you.'

The avalanche of reproaches at least gave the count time to think up some defence; so, when at last Madame de Barthèle paused to take breath he was ready with a pretext which he hoped would get him out of the morass in which he found himself.

'*Mon Dieu*!' he said with a shrug and putting on an air of *sang-froid*, 'Haven't you devined my position and feelings in all this?'

'No, monsieur, I have not, I confess. I am perhaps obtuse in this, and I await your explanation.'

'You surely cannot but be aware', the count pursued, lowering his voice conspiratorially, 'of the sort of woman this is who has enslaved Maurice.'

'Certainly I am: a charming woman, the daughter of the Marquis de Mormant, the schoolfriend of Madame de Neuilly. You see, you cannot accuse me of underestimating my rival.'

'Certainly not,' the count conceded, in his heart delighted that the baroness did full justice to his mistress. 'Nevertheless, she is a person known to many people, too well known, in fact, despite her birth and manners, and in a way which hardly absolves her from blame.'

'Eh, *mon Dieu*! Doesn't one come across women who lead more scandalous lives than Madame Ducoudray every day?'

'That may be,' the count returned. 'But while I agree that Fernande is very charming, in view of her questionable social status I shall be more rigorous than you, and state my belief clearly that she should not be permitted to stay the night under the same roof as Maurice and Clotilde.'

'In which case, my dear Count, if that is indeed the reason for your rendezvous with her, I have to inform you that on my request Madame de Neuilly has given orders to her people to return to Paris as she will be staying with us until tomorrow.'

'Must you always be so thoughtless? Can you not see you are running the risk of an almighty scandal?'

'Who is going to make this almighty scandal?'

'Madame de Neuilly for one.'

'Nonsense! Didn't you see how she greeted Fernande?'

'Yes, but only because she understood her to be a respectable Madame Ducoudray. And can't you see? The longer this act is played the more likely she will be to find out who she really is. Then there are Léon de Vaux and Fabien de Rieulle.'

'But what motives could they have for betraying her?'

'Oh, who can say what goes on in the minds of young hotheads like them?'

'Take care, Count, take care! If you go on about them like that I shall begin to suspect you of being jealous of them.'

'And you would be altogether wrong, my dear,' he returned, feeling a renewed accession of tenderness for his former mistress. 'I am thinking only of Maurice and Clotilde.'

'And that is precisely why I am keeping Madame Ducoudray overnight. So you see we both have the same object in view. See how reasonable I am when things are made clear to me! Forgive me for having entertained suspicions of you and Fernande.'

'Oh! What an idea!'

'A terrible idea; for it would be infamous. A crime, in fact.'

'A crime?' the count echoed, taken aback.

'Certainly. You know very well, my dear, that Maurice is really your son.' Her words were followed by what sounded like a stifled cry. Both the count and Madame de Barthèle, startled, turned round, but seeing no one they took their way slowly towards the house, conversing as they went.

* * *

All this while the two friends were strolling around the garden smoking.

'Well, Léon,' Fabien remarked as he watched the smoke of his cigar curl into the air above his head, 'you must admit things are turning out marvellously. All along I have wanted to know who Fernande really was, and thanks to the insufferable Madame de Neuilly now I do. And you have been dying to know who the sovereign ruler of number 19, rue Saint-Nicholas is, and thanks to the confusion and indiscretion of the count, you have discovered that.'

'Without counting the delightful comedy played out all day under our very eyes! You know, my dear fellow, Fernande is a superbly splendid woman, and if I don't have her soon I shall feel like doing another Maurice on her.'

'I wouldn't advise that, my dear chap. I don't think she would do for you what she has done for Maurice.'

'You think she still loves him, then?'

'To distraction. It is obvious.'

'In that case, how come her liaison with the count?'

'Oh, my dear fellow, that is simply one of the mysteries of female psychology. Who is to know? *Mon Dieu*! We have seen going on all around us today a whole drama of emotions. Looking at these people, who would think that behind every one of those faces there is a passion gnawing nicely away at their hearts?'

'Speaking of passion, how is yours getting along?'

'Slowly, slowly. It will take some time to bring it to the boil, I fear. I was on the verge of getting somewhere when that damnable Fernande came along and spoilt it all. If I can do her a bad turn by helping you to make her your mistress, count on me!'

'I'm afraid my position is much the same as yours, and it's going to be a protracted effort.'

'Never mind! Press on! In the meantime let's make an alliance offensive and defensive. You want Fernande, I want Clotilde. So, I will help you all I can if you will do the same for me. Agreed?'

'Done!' The two shook hands on the pact.

'Ssh!' Fabien said as he withdrew his hand. 'Someone's coming.' The someone proved to be Madame de Neuilly. She was walking quickly and with the air of someone bearing important news.

'Ah! there you are, gentlemen!' she greeted them. 'It is very gallant of you, I must say, to leave us women on our own! Fortunately I had no trouble finding you. Your cigars glow like lanterns.'

Both young men instantly threw away their cigars.

'Believe me, madame,' Fabien excused himself and his friend with a false air of gallantry, 'if we had known you wanted us we would have hurried to find you. Have you something to tell us?'

'Have I something to tell you!' the widow repeated mockingly. 'Only that you have really done a charming thing in bringing this *respectable person* into the home of Madame de Barthèle and Clotilde!'

'What do you mean, madame?' Léon demanded. 'Be good enough to explain, please.'

'Oh yes! Pretend you don't understand me! Try to make me believe you don't know who this so-called Madame Ducoudray really is!' The two men exchanged glances. 'But really,' she went on, 'is it so astonishing I should have discovered the truth? That wasn't very difficult, let me tell you. Madame de Barthèle asked me to tell this creature's coachman via her *valet de chambre* to return to Paris on the order of his mistress. I did better than that: I summoned the coachman himself. When I talked to him about Madame Ducoudray he looked amazed and asked who this Madame Ducoudray was. Then I questioned him and got the truth out of him to the effect that she is not a Madame Ducoudray, not married, and called simply Fernande. I am no longer surprised she doesn't want her father's name to be mentioned. I am beginning to see through the whole game now. But what I cannot understand is how Maurice could come to fall in love with one such as her. What times we live in, *mon Dieu*! when young men of good family make themselves familiar with such creatures! If I were in the place of Madame de Barthèle and Clotilde I would know what to say to people who brought this person to Fontenay.'

'You are being unjust, madame,' Léon protested when he was able to get a word in among the torrent that came from the outraged prude. 'It was Madame de Barthèle herself who asked us to bring Fernande here.'

'Ah! I recognise the thoughtlessness of my cousin there. But surely Clotilde …'

'She was in complete agreement,' Fabien put in.

'And yet she knew her husband to be in love with this creature?'

'Perfectly well.'

'And allowed her to go into Maurice's bedroom?'

'It was she who took him there.'

'*Mon Dieu! Mon Dieu*! It is beyond belief! Now I understand why it was I upset the applecart on my arrival. And does Monsieur de Montgiroux play a role in this scandalous act by any chance?'

'Oh yes,' said Léon with a laugh. 'But we must do the worthy count the justice to say that he had no idea he was to meet a Mademoiselle de Mormant here.'

'I can well believe it! What respectable persons are going to associate themselves with women like her? And yet, *mon Dieu*! here am I who have embraced her, chatted with her like a friend and run after her all day! This is what comes of being too good-hearted.'

The two men exchanged a meaningful smile.

'Then we take it you will be depriving us of your company, madame,' Fabien said, 'for I presume you will not wish to find yourself yet again in the same room as your former friend.'

'Doubtless that is what I ought in all conscience to do,' the widow replied in her most vinegary tone, 'and it would be no more than just if I were to give Madame de Barthèle and Clotilde such a lesson. But I am curious to learn how my former friend, as you call her, will behave in my presence now that I know what she is.'

'Presumably as she has done so far,' Léon suggested, 'since she is not aware that you have fathomed her secret – that is unless you or someone else inform her of the fact.'

'And that is just what I intend to do if she has the temerity to address me at all. And I shall be still more curious to see how everyone reacts when we meet in Maurice's room. Ah yes! Now I come to think about it that will really be worth seeing. For if Maurice is in love with this woman, it must mean that he does not love his wife!'

The mere thought of this brought an expression of malevolent joy into the face of the widow and seemed to buoy her whole person, coming as it did as a return for the humiliation she had suffered from the man she had coveted for a husband and the woman who had triumphed over her. The genius of envy instilled a delicious vengeance over her heart knowing that she had the power to crush with disdain her former friend who had constantly shown her superiority over her in the past and was flaunting that same superiority yet again.

Full of joyous anticipation, then, she went along with the two young men towards the house. But on the perron she stopped with, 'Gentlemen, a thought has just come to me. Will you give me a truthful answer if I ask you a serious question?'

'Ask, madame,' Fabien replied.

'Is today the first occasion on which Monsieur de Montgiroux has met this pretended Madame Ducoudray?'

Léon and Fabien looked at each other, struck by the diabolical instinct of the woman.

'I wouldn't like to swear to that,' Léon answered with a meaningful smile.

'I am certain it is not,' she went on. 'Yes, I feel sure they know each other; more, that he has feelings for this woman. I have caught looks on his part which betray him. Ah! that would really be too rich if Maurice and Monsieur Montgiroux ...' And here the widow, caught up in her malicious anticipations, chuckled.

'Too rich?' Fabien repeated, puzzled.

'Or rather, dreadful,' she corrected herself with a sudden change to seriousness. 'Yes, dreadful is the word, in that ...'

'In that?'

'Nothing. Nothing,' the widow prevaricated, obviously nursing an idea she was not prepared to divulge, at least just then. 'We must let things go on as they are and await events. We shall see what we shall see!'

And with a smile of ineffable malignancy she stepped lightly into the house and up the stairs confident in her belief that she now held her victims in the hollow of her hand.

Seven

Seven

While the domestic drama we have laid before our readers was being played downstairs by the persons involved, upstairs the cause of all the brouhaha, namely, Maurice, was lying in bed soothed by the sweet anticipation of seeing Fernande yet again. Doctor Gaston was with him.

'Doctor,' Maurice began in a low voice and looking round anxiously as if making sure no one else was there to hear him, 'now that we are alone, will you explain to me how Fernande comes to be here.'

'For an invalid you are too curious.'

'She came to learn, then, that I was ill.'

'Of course.'

'And my mother agreed ...'

'Naturally.'

'And Clotilde ...'

'The same. But now, Maurice, confess to me, being your doctor, and since they say confession is good for the soul, and in any case mental and physical health are invariably interlinked, do you still love this woman as madly as ever?'

'Ah, don't ask me that, Doctor!' Maurice groaned. 'I try to think of Clotilde, so good, so patient, so kind, but ...'

'Which means that you admire her, but love Fernande.'

'Yes, that's true, Doctor. I can't help it. I have tried to conquer my feelings, which I realise are guilty, but it is impossible. My whole being is bound up with her. When I saw her again just now it was as if I was finding my old self again; as if the air, the sun, my life-blood, everything that seemed to have deserted me, returned all in a moment. If that isn't love, what is?'

'I'm afraid you have a bad dose of the malady.'

'Do your best for me, Doctor,' Maurice appealed with the air of a spoilt child.

'I suppose you mean will I do my best to persuade her to stay. Well, we must wait and hope. The secret of life is to live at all in the first place, to live well in the second, and happily if possible.'

'But that's the problem, Doctor, to live happily without hurting others – in this case my wife and my mother, and that isn't easy.'

'Never mind. Get yourself back to health first of all, then I can try to cure you of your passion!'

'But I don't want to be cured of it!' Maurice argued, raising his voice.

'Ssh! Someone's coming. Perhaps Fernande.'

'No, it isn't her footstep.'

It was in fact Madame de Neuilly, followed by Fabien and Léon. Behind them came Madame de Barthèle, Fernande, Clotilde and Monsieur de Montgiroux. There followed a general movement until finally everyone was seated. Scanning them closely, Maurice tried to discover from their expressions the different emotions which agitated them, and whether from reality or imagination it seemed to him that the mood of those assembled had changed since he had last been with them. Unknown to him, in fact, each one had undergone a significant experience. Clotilde had learned Fernande's history; Madame de Barthèle, despite Monsieur de Montgiroux's denial, had come to suspect an intimacy between him and Fernande, and this suspicion continued to disturb her; Fernande had discovered that Maurice, while bearing the name of Barthèle, was in fact the son of Monsieur de Montgiroux, and the knowledge that she had been the mistress of both father and son worked havoc in her mind; and finally, Madame de Neuilly had ferreted out that Fernande was not Madame Ducoudray at all but merely

Fernande, a courtesan, and further had devined the jealousy of Madame de Barthèle and the feelings of the count for Fernande. Thus for Maurice only his friends Léon and Fabien appeared the same. Fernande was pale and sat with eyes sad and lifeless; the count and the baroness were clearly abstracted while Madame de Neuilly, her eyes shining with a triumphant gleam and her lips curled in a derisive smile, seemed to dominate the company like an evil genius.

At first all went smoothly, everyone exchanging the civilities usual among people on first entering a room; but soon the general conversation dried up, and a fraught silence reigned. Maurice, sensing this, said in a low perturbed voice in the doctor's ear, '*Mon Dieu*, Doctor! What has happened?' Gaston would have given worlds to be able to reassure him but felt unable, himself feeling a new and unknown danger in the atmosphere.

They had grouped themselves so that Fabien was next to Fernande, Léon beside Clotilde, Madame de Barthèle, determined not to allow the count a minute's freedom, close beside him. Madame de Neuilly alone found herself in pointed isolation and so was enabled to distil her mental venom at leisure.

Let me see, her thought ran, let me see if one of these people here will have the decency to speak a word of civility to me. Monsieur Léon is occupied with Clotilde. That is understandable. After all, we are in her house, and I shouldn't be surprised if he isn't thinking to take advantage of her husband's abandonment of her to take his place. Not a bad idea, that! And it will be interesting to see whether my young cousin decides to give her husband a little tit for tat. Monsieur de Rieulle has no thought for anyone except Fernande, a common kept woman. Monsieur de Montgiroux is pretending to listen to Madame de Barthèle's thoughtless chat, but his mind is obviously elsewhere. And here am I, left alone like a leper. Yet with a word I could change the whole scene. I have only to say to Clotilde: 'You are young, beautiful, rich, but you see now that all these things together are not enough to keep a husband faithful, though they may give you lovers.'

To Fernande: 'You have taken a husband from his wife, come here under a false name, are only waiting until Maurice, who is devouring you with his eyes, is better, to continue your adulterous intrigue with him.'

To Monsieur de Montgiroux: 'You play with your politics as you do with love. Blasé with self-permitted pleasure, you stimulate your sensual appetite with a seasoning of incest.'

To Madame de Barthèle: 'This creature you have invited into your house against all propriety and through weakness for your undeserving son, is profiting by your hospitality to take from you the man who for twenty-five years has made you both a source of scandal.'

To Maurice: 'You think yourself happy, and have no idea that your father has supplanted you in your ex-mistress's apartments, if not in her heart, and that your friend is doing his best to do the same with your wife.'

Yes, if I thought fit, I could get my own back on all of you here who have deliberately left me to sit alone. So then – fixing her eyes on the clock – that in fact is what I will do if within five minutes no one comes and sits beside me.

As will be seen, Maurice was not wrong in having fears. Meanwhile different conversations were going on between interested parties. As we have intimated, Léon was next to Clotilde.

'Madame,' he began, in a low voice, mindful of his pact with his friend, 'I am glad to find myself beside you so that I can tell you something that is on my mind concerning my friend. Much as I dislike admitting it, it was I who on the request of Madame de Barthèle took it on myself to invite Fernande to your house. Fabien knew nothing about it. I hope –'

'Monsieur,' she interrupted him in a frigid tone, 'there is no need for you to try to excuse your friend. I know you both sufficiently well, I think, to realise that you have no secrets from one another. You can therefore spare me the

–118–

embarrassment of telling him that from henceforward his return to my house will be displeasing to me and useless to him.' Thereupon with the most gracious smile she left him to take her place beside Madame de Neuilly, leaving Léon stupified. She was just in time. The widow, her eyes fixed on the clock, was no longer calculating in minutes but in seconds.

'Ah, dear Clotilde!' she greeted her in her customary sour-sweet manner, 'how good of you to take pity on my isolation! I am delighted you can find time to spare me a few moments. I have so much to say to you. Since we last had words together, my poor dear, I have learned sad things about my old friend of Saint-Denis. She is not married, she is not Madame Ducoudray, and I am told she is, to say the least, notoriously easy with her virtue.'

'Dear cousin,' Clotilde returned coldly, 'even supposing all you say of her to be true, while she is under our roof I am perfectly prepared to overlook the facts.'

'But my dear, you can hardly overlook the fact that she has quite turned your husband's head.'

'That may well have been the case,' Clotilde rejoined, 'but I am convinced that Maurice will shortly assure me that the fact no longer obtains.' On which she abruptly got out of her chair and went over to sit in another close to the bed as if to find solace in being near her husband.

Meanwhile the baroness was speaking in a low voice to the count. 'My dear,' she said very seriously, 'I have to tell you that now I have had time to reflect, I quite believe what you told me about Fernande.'

The count felt a momentary uneasiness at her words; then recovering his usual *sang-froid* he replied, 'But why should you not, madame, since I swear to you I spoke no more than the truth.'

It will be seen from this that Monsieur de Montgiroux was prolix with his oaths, being somewhere round about his eighth denial.

'So you honestly do not know Fernande?'

'Only by sight, as one does a woman very much *à la mode*.'

'And you are still free?'

'What do you imply by that?'

'That no secret tie binds you to anyone.'

'Only my political duties.'

'Those have nothing to do with what I want to ask from you. Thank you for your confidences. We will finish our conversation at a more appropriate time and place.'

And here the baroness in her turn went to sit beside Madame de Neuilly.

'Well, my dear cousin,' said the widow with an acid smile, 'what is the matter with you? You are looking very pale. Has the count been making confession to you by any chance?'

'What confession?'

'Why, what everyone knows, *mon Dieu*! – that it is his turn to have an affair with my old schoolfriend Fernande, and is the happy successor to Maurice.'

'I do not know whether Monsieur de Montgiroux has a passion, as you call it, for Fernande,' the baroness returned coldly. 'What I do know is that I am marrying him in a month's time and I invite you here and now to the wedding.'

'What folly!' exclaimed the widow, raising her hands in horror.

'It is far from folly,' the baroness answered with dignity. 'It is simply the putting right of a folly in the past which has lasted too long.'

And getting up with the barest acknowledgment she went and joined Clotilde at the bedside. She had scarcely done so when Fernande left Fabien and in turn seated herself beside Madame de Neuilly.

'Ah, dear friend!' the widow greeted her with a sarcastic smile, 'here is a condescension indeed I ought to be grateful for, I am sure! You, the heroine of the day, leaving a handsome young man who no doubt is paying you charming compliments in order to sit beside poor me! Perhaps we can exchange a few confidences. Tell me, what is your husband? Is he young? Is he rich? Does he love you very much?'

Fernande looked at her with a cold severe expression.

'Madame,' she replied, 'if you knew my history you might be generous enough to feel sorry for me and forgive my errors. I cannot defend myself. But I have been called into this home to try to undo the evil I once committed towards it, and that should help to mitigate your ill-feeling for me.'

Here the courtesan, sustained by her grief and at the same time by the knowledge of her victory over herself, went over to the piano and played and sang that masterpiece of melancholy, the 'Romance' from Rossini's *Saul*. Everyone in the room, even the venomous Madame de Neuilly, listened spell-bound.

Just as Fernande finished, the clock struck eleven.

* * *

This intrusive noise, breaking the silence following the music, destroyed the rare magic of the moment. This was the voice of time reminding of more earthly things and human passions. Madame de Neuilly was the first to break the chain of silence wound about the listeners. Ill at ease in the aura of enchantment inspired by Fernande's performance, she felt the onus on her to display her power over the rest in the mundane matters of the moment, especially as for the first time in her life she had been left without a reply to another woman's challenge, and that woman Fernande! For these reasons she decided that it was time to take her departure. But Madame de Neuilly's shots were Parthian in their character, being the more dangerous for being fired in apparent retreat.

'Eleven o'clock!' she cried, rising to her feet. '*Mon Dieu*! dear cousin, how the time flies when one is with you! And when I think that the hour hand has gone the round of the clock since I arrived! But our invalid needs rest, does he not, Doctor Gaston?'

The doctor nodded his assent.

'I leave you, then, dear Maurice,' the widow pursued, 'with my best wishes for your return to health and strength, which I am sure will not be long now that you are being shown such disinterested devotion. *Au revoir*, dear cousins, and Monsieur de Montgiroux. Madame Ducoudray, I presume, will be staying on since her carriage has been sent back. I have kept my poor rented thing, and if Messieurs de Rieulle and de Vaux will deign to accept places in it, such as it is, I shall be delighted to travel under their safeguard. Not that I fear any misadventure, thank heaven! But strange things happen at night, and in the dark someone might mistake me for Madame Ducoudray and run off with me.'

Unable to escape the onerous duty so put on them the two young men, biting their lips, prepared to take their leave while the widow waited a moment in the anticipation of a farewell embrace on the part of Clotilde and Madame de Barthèle. On seeing that both the women contented themselves with a distant reverence, she made her own adieu in the same manner. Fernande, seated at the piano, barely raised herself from the stool to give an even chillier acknowledgment of her departure.

Scarcely had Madame de Neuilly, accompanied by the two young men, gone than a general atmosphere of embarrassment superseded. Left, as it were, *en famille*, with the need to preserve a front for the benefit of outsiders, those still with Maurice came under the full force of reality. Fernande above all, as the one outsider, suddenly felt overwhelmed by discouragement.

'Madame,' she appealed at last after a silence and in a low voice to the baroness, 'I hope I have given you proof of my willingness to act as you desired. Is there anything more I can do before I retire for the night? I must confess I am more than ready for some rest.'

Her question put the dowager into an awkward state of mind. No longer in any anxiety about the health of her son, and with her mind full of the warnings of the count, with the egoism of all humankind she had been toying with the idea of asking Fernande to return home. It was then, as she showed signs of hesitation, that Clotilde, with the more generous impulse of the young said, 'It is for me now to do the honours to our guest. Maurice,' she continued, turning to her husband, 'it is gone eleven o'clock. You need your sleep. We are going to leave you to settle down.'

Silence in certain situations can be more eloquent than any words. An appealing sigh and look was the only response of the invalid, but both perfectly understood by the two young women. All rose to take their leave with the exception of Monsieur de Montgiroux who, a prey to agitating and contradictory purposes and emotions, did not get out of his armchair.

'Count,' Madame de Barthèle observed, 'don't you agree it is time we retired for the night and left Maurice in peace after such a trying day?'

The peer, pulled out of his feverish somnolence, got out of his chair with some indistinguishable words, and after shaking Maurice's hand and bowing to the ladies, left the room, to be followed by them after each in turn had bidden the invalid goodnight. And soon, with each one in his room, night and silence descended on the château with apparent calm after so dramatic a day.

But this calm was only superficial. Each of the inmates had his or her problems, agitation of mind, confused vibrant emotions.

To begin with the count. Now on the threshold of old age he had come to see in Fernande a last hope of happiness, and as old men do, he clung to that hope with a passion which burned with its final flame. The courtesan had become the prime necessity of his life, and to possess her he was prepared to go to any length, even to that of marrying her. 'If I marry her,' he reasoned as he sat on his bed, 'it will be the means of making my last years at least years of happiness. And then, when she has got over the shock, Cornélie will understand that by doing this I shall have been the means of putting Fernande out of Maurice's reach and so sending him back to Clotilde. As for what society will have to say, well, I have devoted forty years of my life to my country, and anyway my private life is my own affair. The marriage will be a month's wonder and then forgotten. But all this planning is useless until I have had it out with Fernande. I must see her at once and put my mind at rest.'

Madame de Barthèle for her part was turning similar yet very different notions over. Until now she had been content in the knowledge of her power and claims over the count stemming from their liaison, never doubting that at his age he would have no wish to stray from her influence; but with the suggestive remarks of Madame de Neuilly rankling in her memory she was less confident, and her impulsive nature led her on to make desperate plans to prevent him from breaking the ties which had so far bound them ... In addition to which, she reflected as she sat in her room, it is only right that I should make sure of keeping his fortune in the family rather than see it go to some woman of his ageing fantasies. But I must get his word at the earliest possible moment before the fickle creature can change his mind. Let me see – with a glance at her watch – it is now nearly half-past eleven. By midnight everyone should be asleep. His room is next to mine. I will go and settle things with him. The sooner the better!

Clotilde was no less agitated than Madame de Barthèle and Monsieur de Montgiroux. Since the morning she had been initiated to new emotions and unbelievable circumstances. That light covering of coldness which had until then controlled her heart had been melted by the heat of jealousy, and this in turn had engendered unknown passions threatening now to consume her whole being.

Finally, Fernande. When at last she found herself alone in her room except for her maid, she breathed more freely.

'Mademoiselle,' she said, 'I shall not undress. I have no wish to sleep, so I shall manage without you. Only, I should be glad if you would find out whether my *valet de chambre* is still here.'

'Yes he is, madame. Only the coachman has left with the carriage. I think he is in the office, waiting for madame's orders.'

'Be good enough, then, to get him for me, mademoiselle. I have orders for him.'

The maid left, and Fernande waited, leaning pensively against the mantelpiece. A few minutes later the *valet de chambre* knocked and entered.

'Ah, *mon Dieu!*' he cried, 'Is madame not well?'

'What makes you say that, Germain?'

'You are so pale, madame!'

Fernande looked at herself in the mirror and saw that Germain had good reason for his alarm. After being on the rack all day her features, now that she was alone, had relaxed, only to betray a profound emotional reaction.

'No, it is nothing, Germain, thank you,' she said, forcing a smile. 'I am very tired, that is all. Now, listen carefully. I want you to do something for me, something most important and which will need all your discretion.'

Here she went over to the window, lifted one of the curtains and looked out. 'The night is clear', she said going back to him, 'and the village is not far. I want you to leave the house and return without anyone knowing. Go to Fontenay, hire a carriage, coach, coupé, any available means of transport regardless of cost, and arrange for the driver to wait for me at the end of the avenue. Can you do this?'

'Certainly, ma'am. But then what?'

'Stay down below, in the ante-room, and wait for me there. I will join you as soon as I am ready.'

'Very good, ma'am.'

Left alone, Fernande gave way to the grief she had kept at bay for so long. Had she not good cause for her tears? Within twelve hours she had learned two terrible truths: that Maurice still loved her, and that Monsieur de Montgiroux was his father. Placed between the two, she could no longer look at either without the horror of incest raising its terrifying head. 'From now on', she said to herself, 'my future must be radically changed, my past life obliterated. I need peace, and if possible, forgetfulness. My soul must not become tainted like my body has been.'

She was at this stage of her reflections when there was a knock at her door, and on her 'Come in' Maurice's *valet de chambre* entered, a letter in his hand. She took it and read:

> I have returned to life and health through you, and for you, Fernande. I must see you so that we can discuss our future. Come to my room and complete the cure you have begun. I have told you a hundred times my love for you can end only with my life, and tell you here and now that my existence can only go on with my love. Come and talk to me.
>
> Maurice

'Tell Monsieur de Barthèle', Fernande said to the valet, 'that I will be with him in ten minutes.'

When the door was closed behind him she collapsed into a chair, utterly overwhelmed, heart-sick, prostrated.

* * *

She remained so, incapable of movement, for several minutes, unconscious of time, only roused by a knock on her door which opened to reveal Monsieur de Montgiroux. His visit was so little expected that she could not repress a start approaching terror.

'You, monsieur!' she cried. 'What do you want with me at this hour?' She was quite unaware of course of the preliminaries which had finally brought the count to her room; that Madame de Barthèle, intent on carrying out her plan, had opened her door just in time to see the count stealthily making his way along the passage, candle in hand; that realising at once that he was making for Fernande's door she had immediately returned to her room and by devious stairs and passages known to her was now in the dressing-room attached to Fernande's bedroom where, her ear glued to the thin partition and simmering with jealousy, she prepared to overhear what passed between her and the count.

'Surely you understand my impatience to see you after

waiting all day and after your failure to keep our rendezvous,' the peer replied in answer to her question.

'It would surely have been better for you to have waited until we were in a different place and time, monsieur. But I appreciate the necessity for us to reach a clear understanding together. Speak then; I am listening.'

In saying this Fernande, taking pity on the unusual emotion shown on the face of the ageing count, invited him to take a chair close to her; whereupon he placed his candle on a small table nearby and seated himself. A long silence ensued.

'I told you I was listening, monsieur,' Fernande said.

'Madame,' he began uncertainly, realising a longer silence would be ridiculous, 'you have come here –'

'Say rather that I was brought,' she interrupted him. 'You surely understand I had no idea where I was being taken.'

'Yes, madame, I realise that. But by what diabolical combination of events *mon Dieu*! were you brought here? And what do you intend now may I ask?'

'To leave this house this very night, never to return.'

'You are serious, then, in renouncing Maurice?'

'Yes, serious is the word,' Fernande confirmed in a voice of profound grief.

'For ever?'

'For ever.'

'You are an angel!' the count exclaimed, moved almost to tears.

'You exaggerate, monsieur,' she said with a sad smile.

'Not a whit, my dear, not a whit! Now then,' the peer continued, marshalling his thoughts and hopes, 'you asked me why I have come to you at this hour rather than wait for a more seemly time and occasion. The truth is, Fernande, I can't wait. My heart is torn with longing for you. All today you have been so wonderful, so true, so compassionate, and I have come to appreciate you at your true worth.'

Fernande could not repress another sad smile at this impassioned outburst of the peer so out of character to his normal demeanour; but understanding the danger of allowing herself to be softened by his words, she immediately hardened herself and hid her feelings under a cold and dignified manner.

'Well and good, monsieur,' she responded, 'but all that does not explain what you hope to gain from prolonging this interview.'

'What! Don't you understand that I love you, love you with all the sensibility of a man of my age? that you have become a necessity of my life? that I cannot live without you? And don't you realise that the events of today must either separate us or unite us? So now, knowing the facts about your birth and the uprightness of your heart, and admiring your marvellous talents, I have come to ask you to become united to me in all the decency of religion and the law – in a word, to be my wife. Fernande, share my fortune and my life.'

Fernande, though touched by the obvious sincerity of the count's appeal, forced herself to keep up her self-imposed role.

'Believe me, monsieur,' she replied, 'I appreciate the honour you have done me by your offer. But have you not reflected on the impossibility of it?'

'What impossibility?'

'First, your social position, your political career. What do you suppose the world will say to your marriage with a courtesan?'

'I do not care a straw for the world's opinion. And besides, a husband always has the advantage of raising his wife to his own social status.'

'Then in addition you will be denying your heritage to your niece and your s— nephew.'

'Maurice and Clotilde will come into three millions one day.'

'Then again,' she continued pitilessly, 'you seem to forget that Madame de Barthèle has prior claims on you. Your honour and her peace of mind demand your first consideration of her.'

'All that is nothing, Fernande. I love you, not Madame de Barthèle.'

'Lastly', she insisted, 'and most importantly, do you see nothing else which makes our union impossible?'

'Nothing, except your refusal.'

'Reflect. Think, monsieur le comte.'

'All my reflections are made. At my age one does not commit oneself to anything lightly.'

'In that case, believe me I am grateful for the offer you have so honourably made me …'

'But you do accept, Fernande? Tell me: do you accept?'

'Tomorrow you shall have my answer. Tonight I need to be left alone. Leave me to think it over, I beg you.'

Fernande's injunction was too strong to be contested. The count bowed, picked up his candle and left in all the agitation of uncertainty.

Madame de Barthèle had not lost a word of the conversation, and realised that an alteration of her plan of campaign was necessitated. Since her former lover was so besotted on the courtesan as to be prepared to scandalise society by marrying her, she understood it would be useless to appeal directly to him. Second thoughts told her to address herself to Fernande, to appeal to her not so much for herself as for the sake of her son and daughter-in-law. After waiting for some minutes she retraced her steps. But on reaching Fernande's door she found it open, and inside, instead of Fernande, Clotilde.

'Whatever are you doing here?' she demanded in astonishment. Then realising the need to explain her own presence there, 'I came just to make sure that Madame Ducoudray was all right,' she said. 'She looked far from well when she left us. But she is not in her room, I see.'

'But why isn't she in her room?' Clotilde demanded as much to herself as to Madame de Barthèle. 'You know very well why she isn't here. She has gone to Maurice's room.'

'To see Maurice!' Madame de Barthèle expostulated. 'Why would she want to see Maurice at this time of night?'

'Don't you understand?' Clotilde rejoined in a voice made harsh and accusing by jealousy. 'She loves him and he loves her.'

Madame de Barthèle was too preoccupied just then to observe the pallor of face or note the strident voice of her daughter-in-law.

'I don't believe it!' she declared.

'But I know it!' Clotilde cried as she seized the other's arm with a force which made her look more attentively at her daughter-in-law.

'Well, even suppose she is with Maurice, what is there in that to upset you so?'

'But can't you understand? I love Maurice! Can't you see that I resent this woman who has taken him from me?'

The confession came from the young wife in an explosion of words and feeling.

'You, Clotilde, jealous?' The exclamation was uttered by Madame de Barthèle, who knew only too well the meaning of jealousy, in a tone almost of fear.

'What is there astonishing in that?' Clotilde said looking at her companion with eyes inflamed by unconcealed passion.

'But I didn't know –'

'Neither did I,' Clotilde interrupted. 'Until today I didn't know that this woman filled all his thoughts, took up all his heart, could put him at death's door by rejecting him and revive him merely by coming to see him. Well, now I do know it. And they are together at this moment I tell you!'

'But yesterday, my dear, you accepted the necessity of her presence here; you knew they were in love with each other.'

'Yes, but I didn't know I should come to feel I want him as much as I do. Oh yes, I realise now. The fault has been mine. I haven't loved him as I ought to have done, as she loves him, in fact. But now I do. And that is why I must go to his room and see –'

'Wait, wait!' Madame de Barthèle cried, holding Clotilde by the arm. 'Think before you act. Remember, Maurice is not yet out of all danger.'

'The danger is a different one now, and a greater one, I tell you. Come with me …'

'My dear, before you go – think. I have had more

experience than you in such matters. Be careful before you incur an open rupture with your husband. The first quarrel can be the door which lets in all the others. And then, remember: this woman came here only under sufferance, and if you hurt her feelings she may well decide to turn against you instead of putting things right.'

'They love each other! They are in love!' Clotilde repeated blinded by her jealousy, 'and they are alone together!'

'What of it?' the baroness remarked in her most soothing voice. 'They are behaving quite innocently, I am sure.'

Clotilde's lip curled in an expressive manner.

'I understand your feelings,' the baroness conceded, noticing the fact. 'Very well, then. Let us find out for ourselves.'

'But how?'

'You know there is an alcove just behind the bed. We can hide in there and listen.'

'But supposing we find he is still deceiving me with her ...'

'Now listen, my dear. I have a better opinion of Madame Ducoudray than you have. Come with me. I will vouch for everything.'

'But if they are deceiving me!' Clotilde cried despairingly. 'Oh! He has never really loved me! I know that now!' She broke into strangled sobs.

'Come, my child,' urged the baroness who, in the innate goodness of her heart, forgot her own troubles in the newly awakened grief of her daughter-in-law. 'Pull yourself together. You must learn to take control of yourself in circumstances like these.'

And with this injunction, taking Clotilde by the hand she led her half resisting and fearful to the alcove adjoining Maurice's room.

Eight

Eight

Clotilde was not deceived. As soon as Monsieur de Montgiroux had left her, Fernande, keeping her promise, made her way to Maurice's room without fear, shame or hesitation, knowing the duty she had to perform there. As she entered it the clock struck midnight. A new day had begun for the world; for Fernande a new life.

A night-lamp shed its dim light across the room. She found Maurice sitting up in bed, tense, waiting, listening for the appearance of the woman he loved, his mind a turmoil of conflicting emotions. As she appeared at the bedside their glances met, reflecting in silence the strain, the mysterious affinity of their hearts. Fernande, although outwardly calm, was racked with despair as she thought of the pain she was about to inflict on her lover, and stood speechless, empty of words. Maurice too could only look at her in mute surmise. Fernande was the first to break the silence. 'You wanted to see me, Maurice, and I have come,' she said briefly, trying to harden her voice.

'Oh, Fernande!' he replied, 'Now at last we are alone. I want to tell you everything. Oh God! how I have suffered since you left me!'

'I see that only too well,' she answered, softening. 'But at least you have been able to suffer alone and in silence. But I have had to keep up appearances, in the midst of so-called pleasures and gaiety. You have at least eased your heart in tears, while I have been forced to hold my head high and smile through it all.'

'Fernande, you speak like a different person from the one I used to know. You frighten me.'

'You are right, Maurice. I am a different person. Shall I tell you why?'

'Yes, yes, tell me, for heaven's sake.'

'It is simply that your mother has welcomed me as if I were her daughter, and your wife like a sister.'

Maurice shuddered and raised himself on an elbow. 'What do you mean by that,' he demanded. 'What are you trying to tell me?'

'Your voice tells me you have understood what I have to say. You must be prepared, Maurice. We must both be strong.'

'No, no! Not that!' he cried, flinging himself back and twisting his whole body as if in pain.

'Maurice!' she appealed. 'Please, please don't take it so badly. You will make yourself ill again just when you are getting better. If you want me to stay with you and hear what I have to say you must be quiet, and keep calm. I am here to exert authority over you, not only in your own interest but in that of your wife and mother.'

'In that case,' he replied, staring blankly at the ceiling, 'tell me quickly so that I know the worst.'

His tone and movements warned her of the misery she was about to inflict, and to take the greatest care. Leaning down to him as she sat on the bed she took his feverish hands in her own and braced herself to break her inflexible decision to him.

And all the while, the two women in the alcove did not lose a word.

'Maurice,' she began in an unsteady voice, 'let me tell you something – something I shall never forget, nor you, I hope. It is, simply, through your love I have known the happiest months of my life. I see now that it was too perfect to last. When I found you had deceived me, something broke in me. I became terrified of being alone, of silence, of hours passed remembering. So to numb myself I went back to the life I had been leading before I knew you – yes, the so-called life of the courtesan, a life of cynical vice.'

'But I can understand that, Fernande,' he protested as with eyes suspiciously bright he returned the pressure of her hands. 'I understand, and am prepared to forgive and forget.'

'I accept the forgiveness, Maurice, but not the forgetting. That is impossible.'

'But why, *mon Dieu*! why?' he demanded passionately.

'Because our liaison was not one of those banal affairs that are broken and then renewed by caprice. What we felt for each other can never be felt again, be repeated by the mere wish.'

'Oh, *mon Dieu, mon Dieu*!' he almost shouted, raising himself half out of bed as he began to see Fernande's drift. 'Don't talk in that way, Fernande. Don't you realise you are my only hope of happiness? Do you want to ruin that? To destroy me again?'

'Please, Maurice, please, try to keep calm and listen to me. Be brave, and face the inevitable. A return to our liaison is impossible. First,' she went on over-riding his protesting gesture, 'because I am no longer worthy of your love. Secondly ...'

'Well, secondly?' he repeated as she paused, unable to find the words she needed.

'Secondly ... because of the lover I took after you. You do not know his name?'

'No; nor do I want to know it.'

'But you must, Maurice, you must. That lover is Monsieur de Montgiroux.'

'The count!' Maurice cried sitting up with an explosion of energy which alarmed her. 'Oh no! Not the count!'

'Yes, Maurice, the count. You see now the impossibility of it all, I hope. But then', she continued, wringing her hands in her agony, 'how was I to know he was your father?'

'But who has told you he is my father?' he demanded hoarsely.

'Forgive me, Maurice, for mentioning it. I neither

denounce nor accuse anyone. I happened to hear your mother speaking to Monsieur de Montgiroux himself yesterday afternoon.'

Maurice, pale and overcome, fell back into the bed. A long and fraught silence ensued.

'So you see, Maurice,' Fernande resumed at last in a voice she tried to make firm, 'that what you wish – what we both wish – is impossible now. For a moment, I confess, I had a fleeting hope, in spite of the presence of your wife and mother. But you see: every unworthy thought brings its own punishment. I had scarcely indulged the hope when I learned the fatal secret. And I must tell you more. This very evening the count has been to me and offered me his name and fortune. Fernande – la Comtesse de Montgiroux! Can you imagine it! All the same, I listened to him. I felt sorry for him, and in a way admired him – an old man offering me his name in the teeth of a society which would have laughed at him and called him a fool. Think too, Maurice, of your wife. Clotilde is young, younger than I am, beautiful and made to be loved and cherished.'

'I know that. But compared with you she is a statue, without passion. She doesn't know the meaning of real love.'

'That may well have been true yesterday, but not today or the future.'

'What do you mean by that?'

'I mean that yesterday she went through a harrowing experience, a rough awakening, and it has changed her. She now knows what jealousy is, and that has transformed her. I know. I have seen her and spoken to her. She loves you and is worthy of your love, Maurice. Don't throw it away. It would be sacrilege. But in any case, before everything else, over and above all, there is the relationship between me, you and your father. Surely you understand that, Maurice?'

Before Fernande's devastating logic Maurice could only remain in an agony of silent torment. Understanding his suffering through her own, Fernande once again took his hands in hers, and in silence they mingled their tears and their stricken hearts.

'So, Maurice? ...' she ventured at last.

'Yes, this must be the end, I suppose,' he acquiesced through a sob. 'But oh God! how cruel necessity can be!'

'Too true that, Maurice, and for others besides us. But see now,' she went on, desperately trying to salvage some consolation from the wreck of their hopes. 'It was not for nothing I came here. Think of your wife and mother.'

'I accept,' he said heart-brokenly, adding 'but on one condition.'

'What condition?'

'That you promise to see me again, sometime.'

'I promise – if and when you can tell me you are happy.'

He gave a sad smile at her feminine prevarication. Then, 'But you?' he said. 'What are you going to do?'

'I understand you, Maurice' she said, smiling sadly in her turn. 'You are tormented by the idea of seeing me in the company of another man, of my taking another lover, in fact. Yes? There is no need for you to hide it,' she went on reading confession in his face. 'I flatter myself it is your love that speaks as well as your jealousy. So, Maurice, I vow to you here and now: I will never belong to another man. I swear it.'

'Dear Fernande!' he exclaimed softly, his eyes brightening. 'You are an angel! And to think I must lose you! No, no! Impossible!'

'You say that at the very moment when you know in your heart it must be so.'

He had no answer to this, proof that she had divined his thought.

'But are you going to renounce all society, Fernande?' he asked after yet another silence.

'What do you mean by society, Maurice? If you mean the best society, so-called only because it preserves appearances, well, you must know I can't go back to that. If you mean that in which I lived without scruples before meeting you, that is even more revolting to me. No; there can be no more society for me now.'

'But what will you do then? Will you stay in Paris?'

'No. I shall leave.'

'For where?'

'Ah! That is my secret.'

'What! Do you mean I shan't know where you are or what you are doing?'

'Listen Maurice. I understand your wishes, your feelings. I promise that when I am settled I will write to you and give you a full description (but no name) of my place and my doings. In that way you will be able to see me with the eyes of imagination – until the time when you forget I ever existed.'

'Oh, that's impossible! I can never forget you, Fernande. Never!'

'I will believe you, or pretend to believe you. And now – now that all has been said – goodbye, Maurice.'

Maurice, bereft of words, could only utter a sigh of desolation as he fell back with a sob on to the pillow. For a brief moment their eyes, humid with tears, met, took in the other's face for the last time. Then Fernande rose, turned and left him to the solemnity of the night and the heartache of self-imposed resignation.

* * *

On the way back to her room Fernande was overtaken by the baroness and Clotilde.

'Forgive us for listening,' the dowager exclaimed breathlessly. 'We heard everything. Bless you! Bless you!' And carried away by her gratitude she actually embraced the astonished courtesan before she could make any protest, to be followed likewise by Clotilde. Deeply moved, Fernande could only murmur, 'No, no! It is for me to wish you happiness; and I hope the future will make amends for the past trouble I have brought into your home.'

The two women then left her, and she returned without further incident to her bedroom. There, after looking round her in a last and sad goodbye she draped herself in her shawl, took up her hat and hurried down to the hall where her *valet de chambre* was awaiting her.

'Well, Germain,' she said, 'did you manage to find anything?'

'Yes, madame. It is waiting just outside the gate. I'm afraid it is only a one horse chaise, but it was the best I could do.'

'No matter. Let us be off!'

Germain led the way, and after being let out by one of Madame de Barthèle's servants via a side door into the garden, they found their way to the waiting vehicle. Once on the way, lost in thought and memory as she was, she became oblivious of time, only coming back to the present on arriving at her own door. To the surprise of her maid she declined to go to bed; instead, warmed by a blazing fire and a hot drink, she seated herself at a desk and wrote to her solicitor informing him of her desire to see him that same day.

Day broke. While Germain was on his way to the notary with her message she instructed her maid to get together her clothes for a departure of several weeks.

'Is madame leaving, then, at such short notice?' the maid asked in astonishment.

'By ten o'clock I want to have left Paris, Louise.'

'But surely madame could have warned me in advance,' Louise protested with the tenacity peculiar to servants.

'And why so, Louise?' Fernande demanded.

'Because I haven't had time to make preparations for myself, madame.'

'I shall not be taking you, Louise.'

At this abrupt explanation the poor woman's eyes filled with tears; for Fernande, though never allowing herself to be familiar with her servants, was a thoughtful mistress, and they adored her.

'Oh, madame!' Louise cried, 'Have I done anything to displease you?'

'No, not at all, Louise,' Fernande replied, touched by the

girl's concern. 'On the contrary you have always shown yourself devoted and zealous, and I have left instructions about you and the others with my notary.'

'But still, madame, there is something I need to know. When monsieur le comte calls, what am I to tell him?'

At the mention of the count Fernande blushed in spite of all her efforts; then, controlling her emotion, she said, 'Tell him I have left Paris never to return. Now,' she pursued, 'make a single bunch of all my keys and let me have it.'

This done, after telling Louise she wished to be left alone, Fernande unlocked the drawer of a rosewood desk, took out a white satin sachet embroidered with pearls and put it in the bosom of her dress. This perfumed bag held the letters Maurice had written her during their liaison. Then she relocked the drawer, opened an escritoire, turned out and burned all the papers in it, took a pocket-book containing six thousand francs in notes and then waited impatiently for her carriage to take her to the notary's ....

Almost at the same time as she left Paris via the Fontaine gate, Monsieur de Montgiroux entered the city by the Du Maine barrier. He had been unable to wait until the hour agreed on with her and came hot-foot to discover the reason, clear to everyone else, for her disappearance from the château. But he arrived at Fernande's apartments only to find the servants in amazed conjecture and no wiser than himself, and could not bring himself to believe the message passed on to him by Louise. In despair he went round to Madame d'Aulnay's, but even that know-all of the gossip front could not tell him anything of his vanished mistress. However, thanks to her, and to Léon de Vaux and Fabien de Rieulle, all Paris was eventually informed of the sudden and incredible disappearance of the beautiful and renowned courtesan, an event which had the dubious privilege of making the highlight of social gossip for a week: only to be superseded by the announcement of the marriage of Monsieur le Comte de Montgiroux and Madame la Baronne de Barthèle for the 7th June, that is to say one month to the day after the dramatic visit of the courtesan to Fontenay-aux-Roses.

Some three months following the wedding Maurice received Fernande's promised letter in which, without naming the location, she gave him a long and detailed description of the country house and environs in which she had finally come to rest, together with a full report of her daily occupations. She had learned, she concluded, through her 'spies', of the wedding, and of his exploits at the Champ de Mars races, and of Clotilde's obvious new-found happiness, and ended the letter, 'So you see, Maurice, all has turned out for the best. May your future be long and happy! Your Fernande.'

* * *

Three years later still, on returning from mass at the local church, she found her steward and general factotum, Jacques, waiting for her in an unusual state of perturbation.

'What is the matter, my good Jacques,' she enquired, 'and why all this agitation?'

'The fact is, madame,' the old peasant replied, 'something very strange has happened while you were away.'

'Tell me, then,' she said, smiling.

'Well, madame, a young man on horseback came trotting along the avenue and asked me if I could direct him to Monsieur Savenay's place – you know, about a couple of kilometres away. I told him; but then, instead of going away he looked at the house and the avenue in a strange way. Then he said 'Who does this place belong to?'

'To Madame Ducoudray,' I said.

'I thought I recognised it from her description,' he said, and seemed very moved. Then he said he had known you when you lived in Paris, and asked if he might look round the château. I hope I did right, madame, but I saw no reason against it.'

'You did perfectly right, my good Jacques,' she confirmed in a voice which, despite all her self-control, she could not prevent from shaking.

'So he got off his horse and we went inside together. And this is the strange part of it all, madame: he seemed to know his way round, and what each room was used for, though he swore he'd never been here before.'

'Ah!' was all Fernande could say with a deep sigh. Then forcing a voice which still shook a little, 'Did he say anything about himself?' she said.

'No, madame. But he took a notebook from his pocket, tore out a page, wrote something and said, "Here. Take this, and give it to Madame Ducoudray." '

'And have you got it?'

'Here it is, madame.' And Jacques, fumbling in a pocket, produced the sheet. On it was scribbled:

I am happy, Maurice.

A profound sigh escaped her as she read it, and two tears she could not repress ran down her cheeks.